DATE DUE

FEB 1 6 REC'D	DEC 2 2 2011

The Library Store #47-0119

---*bluefish*---

PAT SCHMATZ

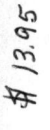

CANDLEWICK PRESS

This is a work of fiction. Names, characters, places,
and incidents are either products of the author's imagination or,
if real, are used fictitiously.

Copyright © 2011 by Pat Schmatz

All rights reserved. No part of this book may be reproduced,
transmitted, or stored in an information retrieval system
in any form or by any means, graphic, electronic, or
mechanical, including photocopying, taping, and recording,
without prior written permission from the publisher.

First edition 2011

Library of Congress Cataloging-in-Publication Data

Schmatz, Pat.
Bluefish / Pat Schmatz. — 1st ed.
p. cm.
Summary: Everything changes for thirteen-year-old Travis, a new
student who is trying to hide his illiteracy, when he meets a sassy
classmate with her own secrets and a remarkable teacher.
ISBN 978-0-7636-5334-7
[1. Literacy—Fiction. 2. Secrets—Fiction. 3. Teachers—Fiction.
4. Middle schools—Fiction. 5. Schools—Fiction.] I. Title.
PZ7.S34734Bl 2011
[Fic]—dc22   2010044815

11 12 13 14 15 16 BVG 10 9 8 7 6 5 4 3 2 1

Printed in Berryville, VA, U.S.A.

This book was typeset in Warnock.

Candlewick Press
99 Dover Street
Somerville, Massachusetts 02144

visit us at www.candlewick.com

*For my two favorite bluefish:
Jeremy Schmatz and Kim Swineheart*

Chapter One

Travis stood in front of locker number 78. The clatter and bang and yammering voices pounded at the back of his head. He started the combination, slowly spinning the dial. Seventeen . . . back to the left . . .

KaBLAM! Something hit the locker next to his head and sent a jolt through him. He whirled, fists up and fight juice flooding. A shoe landed on the floor next to him, new white leather with a dark-blue swoosh on the heel. Travis took a shaky breath in and out and wiped his hands on his pants. He picked up the shoe and looked around.

The hall was full of kids talking, laughing, slamming lockers, and heading toward class, but nobody so much as looked his way. Seemed like the shoe had thumped out of thin air.

Travis leaned against the locker and held the shoe sole-to-sole against his own. It was a size or three smaller and made his ratty Converse edged with swamp mud look like something he'd dug out of a Dumpster.

A head bobbed down the hall toward him, dipping with a one-shoe walk. The guy was small, and Travis figured him for a seventh-grader, maybe even sixth. He had deep brown skin and hair cropped too short to kink, and he carried a nice new over-the-shoulder book bag. He was very tucked in and tidy except for his shoeless left foot. His right foot wore a new white Nike.

Travis waited until the kid passed, then edged up behind him. When he got close enough, he bumped the shoe into the kid's hand. The kid spun around, brown eyes big and mouth open to show a bundle of braces. Travis hustled on past, weaving into the crowd. If it were him, he wouldn't want to have a big chat. He'd just want his shoe back.

First period, Travis settled into a seat on the outside row, halfway back. Social studies, Ms. Gordon. She read down the roll call, made it through to the *W*s, called "Vida," and then tripped all over a last name.

"It's Would-ja-husky," said the girl behind Travis. "My public calls me Velveeta."

"Think cheap cheese," called a tall guy across the room.

"Ms. Gordon, you should know: Chad's kinda damaged," said Velveeta. "He repeats the same jokes over and over. I think it's a condition, but we don't talk about it."

"Shut up, Cheap Cheese." Chad flipped her the bird behind a raised palm.

"All right, enough." Ms. Gordon closed the roll book. "Chad Cormick, come on up here and pass out the textbooks."

Chad dumped a text on Travis's desk as he passed by. It landed with a thud. Heavy. Dense. Travis folded his arms across his chest and dropped his chin. Another school year. No way out.

He slogged through a couple of hours of first-day science and math, the air pressing in hotter and heavier, the walls closing around him. Fourth period was a short one, only thirty minutes. He had reading in Room 134. He hadn't had reading as a separate class since fifth grade.

He stopped in the doorway of the classroom. The entire back wall of the room was a built-in bookshelf, loaded with books. Bookshelves lined the opposite wall. No windows. The ceiling looked lower, the walls closer, than in the other rooms.

Travis backed out, dropped his pencil and notebook in his locker, and headed for the double doors and the rays of sunlight. He pushed the door open, feet moving without stopping.

He turned left, crossed the asphalt parking lot, and

headed out of town. When the sidewalk ended and he was walking on gravel beside the road, he looked over his shoulder. The school building squatted behind him, spread out beyond the cars, too far away to reach out and drag him back.

Travis had run away from school the first day Grandpa left him off at kindergarten, and three more times after that. The fourth time, he got smart and hid in a culvert, so they didn't find him for a few hours. They had to bring the sheriff in, and then Grandpa didn't think it was funny anymore.

You ditch out of school again, and the dog sleeps outside.

Travis hadn't ditched again. Until now. Rosco was gone, so why not?

At the county highway, he took a left, toward the old place. It was more than twenty miles away, but soft white clouds puffed across the clear blue overhead, and a light wind lifted his hair. He untucked his shirt, and the breeze cooled the sweat on his back. A car vroomed by, and a crow hollered from the other side of the road. His feet kept moving, his arms swinging, his body so relieved to be out of the school building that it was worth whatever came after.

Travis had been walking for a long time when the truck crawled up behind him. He knew it was Grandpa without turning to look. Not just the familiar sound of the engine, but the feel of it, the slowing down of it, the ready-to-pounce of it. Grandpa pulled over, got out, and slammed the door.

From the corner of his eye, Travis watched Grandpa stalk across the road. He got ready for Grandpa to step in front of him, shove him back. Then Travis would hit out like he used to in kindergarten, and Grandpa would laugh and slap Travis's hands away like pesky flies.

Only it wouldn't go like that, not anymore. Grandpa knew it, because he didn't step in front of Travis. Instead, he walked alongside, pulling a cigarette out of his shirt pocket.

"Where do you think you're going?" he asked as he lit up.

"Nowhere."

"I can't be leaving work to babysit you."

"So don't." Travis kept walking.

Grandpa grabbed him by the back of his shirt and pulled. Travis went with it, swinging around to face Grandpa, getting a faceful of smoke.

"That hound is not going to be waiting on the porch for you. He's gone, and we don't live there anymore."

Travis turned away from the smoke. He looked out across the fresh-cut hay field on his right. The hay lay in clumps, ready to be baled. Soft. The smell surrounded them. Travis tried to stop the sneeze coming on — he didn't want to give Grandpa that much. He turned away as it blew out of him, breaking the silence.

"Get in the truck." Grandpa flicked his cigarette butt on the ground. "Unless you know someone else who's going to buy your food and put a roof over your head."

And because Travis didn't know anyone like that, he followed Grandpa across the road and got in.

Velveeta on TUESDAY

Hey, Calvin. Hi. I'm in your trailer. When I got home from school, Buttface Jimmy's truck was in the drive, so I came over like always and slipped my key into the keyhole and expected it not to work, but you know what? It slid right in. The door opened.

Everything's exactly the same except for how much you're not here. The empty air in this trailer weighs eighty trillion tons, and it's jumping up and down on my lungs like an elephant on a trampoline. But that beats my creepy brother's wide-alive air any day. I'm going to stay here until he leaves.

Today was the first day of school. The madre was going to give me some money for school supplies, but guess what, she forgot. If you weren't dead, you would've bought me a three-ring binder and a protractor and a calculator.

Your trailer is still the safest and best place I know. Nobody knows I'm here.

If you were here, you'd make me do homework. But you're not here. So who's doing homework? Not me.

Chapter Two

The next day, fourth period, Travis walked into Room 134. He looked around, not knowing if they'd been assigned seats the day before. Everyone else was dropping papers on the podium as they came in. A short, round balding guy with glasses came out of his office at the front of the room, spotted Travis, and walked over.

"Travis Roberts?" he rumbled in the deepest voice Travis had ever heard.

He nodded, and the teacher stuck out a hand.

"Owen McQueen."

His skin was soft, but his grip was hard.

"You can sit there." He pointed to a seat halfway up the first row. "Yesterday you missed my dramatic reading of Billy Collins's poetry, but there'll be more. You also missed your first assignment, a one-pager on the best thing you've ever read in your life. Turn that in tomorrow, please."

McQueen. What a name. He probably got called Queenie when he was a kid, especially if he'd been short and round then, too. But his voice — that was something different.

"Thank you all for your fine papers. I can't wait to read them." McQueen stepped to the front of the room. "I'm supposed to teach you how to take the standardized reading tests so you won't be the child left behind. But because I'm subversive" — he turned and wrote the word on the board as he talked — "(look it up if you don't know what it means, and it will be on the vocabulary test next week), I'm actually going to try to teach you a passion for the written word. Emily Frasher, roll your eyes again in my classroom, and severe castigation will be the inexorable result." He wrote two more words on the board, then turned to face the class. "Between now and the ring of the bell in twenty-two minutes, you are to pick a book from the library wall. Then start reading."

"Mr. McQueen, what if we're already reading something? Can we use that, or does it have to be a book from the wall?"

It was the no-shoe kid, sitting up in the front corner. He was either a grade skipper or a really, really little eighth-grader.

"Excellent question, Bradley Whistler. You may read any piece of literature."

"Define literature," called a girl behind Travis.

"I'll tell you what, Rachel: *you* define literature. All of you. On Friday, please turn in a one-paragraph definition of literature. No copying from Wikipedia. Plagiarism"— he scrawled on the board again—"will have the same result as not turning the paper in — an F. Meanwhile, start reading, and if you can make a case for it being literature, that works for me. Okay, books. Go."

Everyone crowded to the back wall. Travis stayed in his seat until the rush cleared. Then he walked over with his hands in his pockets. The rows were messy, leaning this way and that where books had been plucked out. Paperbacks slid off stacks on the bottom shelf, showing some covers. On one, a fox ran across a snow-covered field. Travis picked up the raggedy book and looked more closely. A tiny hound in the distance of the picture ran behind the fox.

When Travis turned around, he almost bumped into the Velveeta girl who sat behind him in first-period social studies.

"Oops, sorry," she said. "I almost ran you over in my rush to get a book. I bet you took the one I wanted."

He handed it to her. One was as good as another.

"Oh, no, no," she said, waving her hands. "That's not the one I want. I'm sure there's something here that can make me"—she dropped her voice, trying to shove it down as low as McQueen's—"develop a passion for the written word."

She wore a filmy, shimmery scarf wrapped around her gray hoodie, all July-sky blues and deep pine greens. The colors hit Travis like a fresh breath in and out. The girl stepped around him and tilted her head, flicking book spines one at a time with her middle finger as she moved down the row.

"Need help choosing, Velveeta?" Mr. McQueen came up behind her.

"Don't rush me," she said. "Too important to rush."

"Are you a Kjelgaard fan?" McQueen asked, turning to Travis.

Travis shook his head, having no idea what McQueen was talking about.

"The book." He pointed to the fox cover. "Kjelgaard. If you like this one, he's written a lot more. All animals, all outdoors, all the time."

"Oh," said Travis, backing away. "Okay."

He went back to his seat, opened the book, and stared at the first page.

At lunchtime, Travis used his magic plastic card to buy his free lunch: a burger and fries and a cookie. He took the tray to a table in the back corner and sat down. He was about three bites in when a voice came up behind him.

"Hey, mind if I sit here?"

He shook his head, and Velveeta set her tray down across from him.

"Where'd you go yesterday?" she asked. "You were there first period, then gone. Did you puke? Have to go home?"

"No," said Travis. "Had something I had to do."

"Evasive answer. I like that."

She tore open a packet of ketchup and drew a red smiley face on her burger. Then she opened a mustard and added yellow eyebrows and a mustache.

"So what's your story?" she asked.

"What story?"

"Yours. Everybody's got one. You're new. What's yours?"

"No story." He squeezed ketchup on his fries.

"So are you an undercover cop, here to break up a raging crystal-meth ring?"

Travis shook his head.

"Maybe you're an alien, morphed into an eighth-grader so you can infiltrate the human race and learn our secrets."

She waved her hands, erasing that idea before the smile even made it across his face.

"No, wait, I've got it. You're a super-big brain like Matt Damon in *Good Will Hunting*, a secret math genius, right? That's why you don't say anything, because smart math formulas would pour out and they would ship you off to work for the government, right?"

"Nope." The smile feeling dipped back under.

"Okay, I give up. What are you?"

The old third-grade picture of the bluefish popped into Travis's mind, standing beneath the swimming onefish, twofish, and redfish. Just hanging around, leaning on an ocean wave, smiling because it was too stupid to know it was stupid.

"Nothing," he said.

"Well, then, where are you from? Have you ever seen *Old Yeller*? No? It's very old Disney, a classic, about a Travis who lives in Texas. Are you from Texas?"

"No, Salisbury." He finished off his burger.

"Salisbury, Wisconsin? Seriously? Okay, I get it, that's the cover story, because it's so boring no one will question it, moving from one crappy little town to another. You going to eat that cookie?"

She reached across to Travis's tray and took his cookie and held it up in the air, a hostage.

"Hey!"

"Straw is cheaper; grass is free; buy a farm, and you can have all three. Come on. Tell me something. One clue and I'll give it back."

"But it's my cookie."

She looked at the cookie in her hand, then back at him.

"You're right," she said. "Why trust me with your checkered past? I'm a cookie thief. Doesn't exactly inspire confidence, does it?"

She handed the cookie over.

"This school makes the best cookies—it made me lose my mind for a minute. Sorry. I just wanted to make sure you didn't throw it in the garbage. That would be a travesty. Ha. Travesty. Travis."

As she picked up her tray to leave, he broke the cookie in two.

"Here," he said. "You can have half."

She looked directly into his eyes. Like she was reading whatever was written on the back wall of his brain.

"Thank you, Travis Roberts, Mr. Undercover Alien Genius Cop Man," she said. "I think I like you."

She took the cookie half and walked away, her black-and-gray camo pants sagging and dragging on the floor behind her.

Velveeta on WEDNESDAY

Remember how you said there's only two stories: someone goes on a trip or a stranger comes to town? Remember how I went crazy for days, trying to think of a movie that wasn't either of those to prove you wrong? And no matter what I came up with, you figured out some way to make it one of those.

There's a stranger in town, and if you were here asking me "How was school?" and pushing for details every day like you used to, I'd be telling you about him. But you're not here. It's two and a half weeks now of you being more not here every day.

This is morbid, writing to you. Like, what? I'm going to put it in an envelope and write *Calvin Whalen, Dead in Heaven,* and stick it in the mail? Like writing letters to Santa Claus? It makes me feel better, though, coming here after school. Like maybe you're on a long vacation and you'll be home soon. Nothing wrong with pretending, right? Like *The Muppet Movie* song, remember? *Life's like a movie, write your own ending....*

Because I gotta say, I don't like the way this movie is going lately. We need a better writer.

Chapter Three

"Did you do the reading?" Velveeta slid into the seat behind Travis first period.

He shook his head.

"How about McQueen's paragraph on literature?"

He shook his head again.

"Me neither," she said. "Homework is against my religion."

Someone behind them whistled, and Velveeta turned. A couple of girls in the back corner whispered and almost fell over giggling.

"See those girls? They write for *People* magazine, and they've spotted us as the smoking-hot new eighth-grade romance. All we have to do is adopt octuplets, and the paparazzi won't give us any peace."

Travis knew why they were giggling, and it wasn't about octuplets. One of them had corrected his science paper the day before.

"Please turn to page eight of your text," said Ms. Gordon. "You can read a paragraph or just say 'pass' if you prefer not to read. The next person can just pick it up. Megan, will you start us off?"

Travis let out a long, slow breath. The windows were open on the other side of the classroom, and warm air breezed in. Sunshiny bright and cooking up to be another hot one. The swamp would be thick with that baked summer pine-needle smell. Gallons of drool would be sliding down Rosco's sloppy tongue.

"Travis!"

Travis's face flushed hot, and he pretended he was trying to find his place.

"Would you like to pass?" Ms. Gordon asked.

"Yeah, pass," he said.

Velveeta started reading, and Travis relaxed. Her voice motored across the words as if they were a flat, smooth road — no bumps.

At lunchtime, two different groups of girls called Velveeta's name out, but she walked right on by and set her tray across from Travis.

"Look, we're regular lunch buddies now," she said.

"You didn't have one clue where we were in social studies, did you? What were you thinking about?"

"Nothing."

"Do you have a talking quota?" asked Velveeta. "Like, a limit, maybe fifty words a day, and if you go over, you, what, lose your undercover badge? And you can't waste any of them reading out loud in class. Is your limit fifty or only twenty-five? No, no, don't answer — then you'll have to kill me."

"Ten," he said.

"Ha. And you've already used two on me. *Nothing* and *ten*. Better shut up and eat."

He finished off his grilled cheese and started spooning up soup.

"Are you going to eat that cake?"

Velveeta had already finished hers. Travis cut his and handed half across to her.

"Okay, so sometimes the words are not so necesario," she said.

After inhaling the cake, Velveeta sat back and crossed her arms.

"I know what you're thinking. *Why does she pick me?* he wonders. She could be baaing with the popular sheep over there, or shooting baskets in the gym with the jockolas, or outside smoking with the delinks, so why is she sitting with me again?"

She leaned across the table, bringing her nose close to

his. One end of her purple-and-blue scarf trailed on the tabletop.

"Because I saw you give Whistler his shoe back," she said. "That's why."

After the last bell, Travis walked through town, crossing the street so he wouldn't have to pass in front of the big glass window of the bakery where Grandpa worked. He stopped at the bridge and leaned on the railing, trying to find the cardinal that was blasting its lungs out. He scanned the trees alongside the pond and finally spotted it, high in a birch, a hot patch of red in the swim of green.

"Hey, you gonna jump or what?"

Four guys sat on a picnic table in the green space on the other side of the bridge, smoking cigarettes and drinking sodas.

"You need a push?" yelled one of them. "Or a dump?"

"Dump, ha, I'll give him a dump."

"Maddox, you are a dump," said a heavy-shouldered guy with a hint of blond mustache trying to crawl across his lip.

Travis looked closely, measuring them. They must be high-schoolers. He hadn't seen them in the halls, and they were his age or a bit older. The two smaller guys he could take, no problem. Maybe the one called Maddox, too. The blond guy was solid, though, and he had that look. He was the one to watch.

Travis shoved away from the bridge railing and walked past. If they were going to come after him, they'd have to climb the little hill up to street level, and they weren't moving. But their eyes on him wrecked the bird and the water and the color, so there was no point in hanging around. That was the problem with living in town. Someone looked at him wherever he went. Even the houses had eyes, watching every move.

Travis headed up the hill, and as he rounded the curve, the sidewalk ended. The houses became scruffier and farther apart, with shaggy yards and gravel driveways. The paint-peeling yellow box on the right had an empty yard and drive. No old hound standing out front, waving his thin cord of a tail, droopy red-rimmed eyes asking why they'd made him walk the whole twenty miles. Not today. Maybe tomorrow.

Travis fished the key out of his pocket and opened the door. He made a peanut-butter sandwich and took it out to the back stoop. He pushed Grandpa's stinky soda can of soggy butts away and leaned against the house. Three school days down. A zillion left to go.

In the back corner of the yard, a little pine tree tried to scraggle its way up past the shade of the tall wooden fence. The other corner was full of dried dog dookey, and a path was beaten all the way around the perimeter where some trapped dog had run in endless circles.

The front door banged.

"Want a doughnut?" Grandpa called.

Footsteps tromped around the house. Then Grandpa stepped out on the stoop, lighting a cigarette.

"It's a sticker out here," he said. "Musta been hot in school. Want a doughnut?"

"You said that already."

Grandpa looked down and gave Travis a very unsmiley smile.

"Did you manage to stay there all day?"

Travis handed him the butt can. Grandpa sat down and tapped the ash of his cigarette. Then he squinted at Travis through a curl of smoke.

"Everything okay? Teachers and all?" he asked.

Travis shrugged, looking away. Grandpa dragged off the cigarette again, then turned his head sideways to blow out the smoke.

"Can you give it a chance? I miss the woods and the dog, too. But we're both going to have to buck up and make the best of what we've got."

The dull ache chewed on in Travis's chest. Everything he'd ever cared about was gone. Every single thing.

"Okay, don't buck up, then." Grandpa dropped his butt in the can and stood. "Make it as bad as you want. I'm going to the six-thirty meeting. I'll pick you up a burger on the way home."

Footsteps, bathroom door, shower, and Grandpa headed out to his AA meeting. He hadn't had a drink since that hot and horrible afternoon in August when Rosco went missing, but he smoked six times as much, and he was full of useless advice. As if not drinking meant he could tell Travis how to feel.

Travis got up and wandered around the yard, stopping at the little pine in the corner. He ran his fingers over the soft needles. Even if it stretched tall enough to look over the fence, it didn't have anything to look at but another scraggy backyard.

Because I saw you give Whistler his shoe back. That's why. Velveeta's voice slipped in and interrupted the chewing ache. That was the best thing anybody had ever said to him inside a school building.

The neighbors' TV noise rose over the drone of the air conditioner next door. A car backfired on the street. Travis leaned his head against the fence, looking down at the skinny half-bare white pine. He bent over and pressed the green needles to his nose, breathing deeply, trying to fill himself with the smell of woods. The tree had nothing to give.

"It's okay," said Travis, petting the needles like they were Rosco's ears. "Not your fault, trapped here. If I could, I'd dig you up and take you someplace good."

Velveeta on THURSDAY

Your buddy Connie was lying in wait for me after school. When I passed the library, she waved me over like some street-corner drug dealer and offered me a J-O-B. I asked her why, and she said maybe it would make her not miss you so much.

I told her I wasn't going to be joining the old people's canasta club, so forget it. She said she doesn't want me to play canasta. She just wants me to shelve books and do whatever else she says. Five bucks an hour. Four hours on Saturdays and two hours Wednesdays after school.

She said since I'm not fourteen yet, it'd have to be under the table, and she'd pay me in cash and was that okay?

Ha. Is that okay? Now, THAT is funny.

Thirty dollars a week for whatever I want. Maybe I can get the electricity turned back on in your trailer so I can watch movies. Do you know how much torture it's been to not watch movies? I even watched reality TV with the madre last night. That is desperate. That should be a reality show.

Chapter Four

"Today we start individual conferences," said Mr. McQueen in reading. "When I call your name, bring your book into my office and we'll discuss."

He called Heather first. Travis glanced over at Velveeta. She was staring at the cover of a book and playing with the end of her scarf. This one was an October-maple blast of red, orange, and yellow.

Travis traced his finger around the black paw of the fox on the cover of his book. They made such small, neat tracks, those fox paws. One day last winter, he'd followed fox tracks in a new snow and spent all morning tromping circles around the woods and swamp, over brush and under barbwire, until he ended up in a sweat more than three miles from home. He never did find a fox hole.

He opened his notebook and drew fox prints from the upper left to lower right corner of the paper. Then he made some rabbit tracks on the other side of the page.

"Mr. Roberts."

Travis grabbed the fox book and walked to the front of the classroom. He stepped through the office doorway. Stacks and gangs of books and magazines leaned in from every wall, shrinking the small room down to nothing.

"Have a seat." McQueen settled behind the desk.

The pile of books at Travis's feet crowded his legs, making him sit slightly sideways. If all the books in the room jumped him at once, they'd bury him. It would take days to punch his way up through the covers and the pages.

"Let's see the book."

Travis handed him the fox.

"Why'd you choose this one?"

Travis shrugged.

"You like foxes?" McQueen held the book up, tapping the cover.

Travis nodded. The cover of that book was the most open space in the room. Rolling snowy fields and distant pines against a gray winter sky.

"You ever see one in the wild?"

Travis nodded again, remembering the fox pups he'd watched in June. The way they'd rolled and dodged as they wrestled, and that one who'd jumped straight up like a lit furry firecracker.

"What was it like? Did you see it up close?"

"Pups last summer," Travis said. "They were cute."

"Lucky!" McQueen popped his eyes wide. "Not many people get to see that — but you're good at being quiet, blending in. Do you spend a lot of time in the woods?"

"Used to, at our old place."

"Miss it?" McQueen flipped through the pages.

"Yeah."

"Well, if it's woods you like, you picked the right book. Kjelgaard is terrific with outdoor and animal stories, beautiful. I mean, listen to this:

> "Chapter One. The Raider. It was a night so dark that only the unwise, the very young, or the desperately hungry ventured far from the thickets, swamps, and burrows where wild things find shelter in times of stress."

McQueen continued to read in his deep, rumbly voice, and Travis sat back in his chair. McQueen's voice brought a starless winter swamp night to life, with rattling leaves and the movement of a fox through the snow. Travis closed his eyes, shutting out the crowd of books, breathing in the cold, clean air.

McQueen stopped reading, and Travis opened his eyes. The swamp disappeared.

"Nice writing, isn't it?"

The mass of books leaned in from the shelves again, waiting to hear what Travis would say.

"How far have you gotten?" McQueen tapped the cover.

"Not very."

"Anytime you want to talk about it, let me know. Or if you need help with anything."

"Okay." Travis stood and reached for the doorknob.

"Some nice line drawings at the start of each chapter," McQueen said. "Funny how a little thing like that can add to a book."

Travis took the book from McQueen and went back to his desk. He spent the rest of the period paging through and looking at the sketches. The second chapter had a drawing of a hound that looked just like Rosco—floppy jaws, skinny tail, and ribs showing. He wished McQueen would have read more.

The bell rang, and Travis headed for lunch, wondering if Velveeta would sit with him again. Returning the shoe was good enough for two days, but probably not three. He almost knocked into Bradley Whistler coming around the corner into the lunchroom.

"Hey, Travis."

Travis stopped short.

"Thanks for my shoe the other day."

"Sure."

Bradley stood there looking up at him as if he had something else to say, but Travis didn't know what it could be. Bradley was a smart kid, for real. He had his hand up all the time with the right answer or another question, and he went over to the high school for math.

"Well, anyway, thanks. See you around."

Travis nodded, and Bradley went to sit with a group of guys. Travis got in line and loaded up his tray. When he came out, Velveeta was half standing at the back table, and she waved him over.

"Hey, why are you smiling?" she said as he set his tray on the table. "I haven't said anything funny yet. That means you're thinking something funny and not letting me in on it. Not fair, Mr. Confidential Comedy Man. Come on, share."

Travis shook his head, still smiling.

"Maybe you're thinking how beautiful I am, and you're too shy to say. Hey, look, you're blushing! Is that it? You're filled with passion for Velveeta?"

"Shh!" hissed Travis, although no one was paying any attention.

"Interaction! You're actually in there!"

The girl at the end of the table looked up from her book.

"Don't worry, Rural RoboCop." Velveeta lowered her voice. "I won't tell anyone. Unless you keep stonewalling me. If you don't start talking soon, I'll tell everyone you're madly in love with me and you pay me twenty dollars every time I sit with you at lunch. It's my lunchroom prostitution scheme."

Travis's face burned hot-red. Velveeta sat back and drummed her fingers on the table, watching, until his skin was about to explode off his skull.

"Fine," she said. "Keep your funny thoughts to yourself. But don't keep them too long, or I'll get hurt feelings. Hey, you were in there with McQueen for a long time. Did he hypnotize you?"

"What do you mean, hypnotize?"

"McQueen and his hypno-eyes—don't tell me you didn't notice. You ever see *The Jungle Book*, old Disney animation? No? You got something against Disney? Anyway, there's this python, and he hypnotizes his prey by staring into their eyes and swaying back and forth and singing, *'Trust in me.'* That's McQueen, all the way."

As usual, Velveeta polished off everything on her tray in a hurry. When he looked up, she was staring at his brownie. Maybe she sat with him to get the extra desserts. Was he supposed to give up half his dessert every day?

"So, tell me one of your still-water-running-deep thoughts," said Velveeta.

"I don't have any," said Travis.

"Okay, then give me a shallow one."

"I like your scarf."

That popped out all on its own, before Travis could reel it back.

Velveeta's head jerked, as if his words had leaped across the table and slapped her. She blinked a couple of times, then pushed away from the table and walked off without another look at his brownie.

Velveeta on FRIDAY

I had a theory that Travis didn't talk because he's dumb as a post. As of today I am trashing that theory.

I brought the scarves back over here yesterday. You never know when the madre is going to decide she needs a rag to wipe up spilled beer or something. I don't want her touching them — they're mine. They're all shimmery and soft and old-lady-looking, and they go perfect with my gray hoodie. Did you give them to me because you knew you were about to leave? If so, you should have told me so it wouldn't have been such a shock.

Does being dead mean that you don't miss Janet anymore? Your wedding picture is still on the kitchen table. I haven't moved anything.

I remember that time you said, "Velveeta, you may be full of baloney, but you are a realist." I wasn't sure what you meant. Now I know. Dead is dead is dead. You're not watching me. You won't ever read this.

I never talk to anyone else like this. If I don't write it to you, I'll stop thinking this way and I'll turn into whoever I would be if there'd never been a Calvin. I can't even think about how horrible that would be. I can barely even think about tomorrow with no Calvin. Or tomorrow after that.

The madre saw me coming out of here yesterday. It freaked her out. She said it's creepy that I hang out in your trailer. But she said that even when you weren't dead, just old.

Chapter Five

Rosco!

The word tore up from Travis's gut, burning through his chest, but he couldn't get any sound out. His voice caught in the back of his throat, strangling him, keeping him trapped in the dream.

The trees on the path to the swamp wavered and morphed and became the crowded hall of Russet Middle School. A whiff of warm, dense smell let him know Rosco was close, weaving among the sea of legs and sneakered feet. He scrambled behind, trying to catch up. Grandpa stepped in front of him, laughing, and blocked his vision.

Travis shoved, and Grandpa flew back. His head bounced off the lockers, and he crashed to the floor. Blood came out of his ear and trickled down his neck. Suddenly, the hall was empty. No kids, no dog. No smell.

Travis's voice finally came out in a squeaky whimper, waking him. His heart hammered, and he lay there, sweaty and shivery, alone, no warm stinky dog weight at the foot of his bed. A soft light shone through the yellow towel he'd stapled around the curtain rod. Cool fingers of breeze stretched through the half-open window, and the birds hollered a racket outside. The house was quiet — Grandpa left early for the bakery on Saturdays.

Travis got dressed, opened the front door, and looked out on the day. Five houses in view, all with their empty eyes looking back at him. He grabbed a jacket and a day-old muffin, took a right out of the driveway, and headed away from town. He took another right, turning onto a narrow asphalt road with no centerline. By the time he finished the muffin, the houses had thinned out and dropped off to nothing. No cars, either, just his feet scuffing along the gravel shoulder. Cornfields stretched on either side of the road.

Travis hadn't gone for a walk since they'd moved, unless you counted his runaway from school. That day, he'd been in the same not-thinking place he went in a fight — no planning or figuring or feeling. Sometimes his body just did things on its own.

Like in the dream, when he shoved Grandpa. The pain

and panic of letting Rosco slip away through the crowd had been so real. Not the everyday dull-tooth chewing in his chest, but sharp like the morning cold where the sun hadn't touched yet.

If only he had taken Rosco with him that morning a few weeks ago. "Stay," he'd said, knowing he was more likely to see the fox pups if Rosco wasn't along. Rosco had flopped in the driveway and watched him go, sad-eyed. And Travis hadn't even seen the pups, just a few chipmunks and a woodpecker. On his way home, he'd given the high-low whistle, expecting Rosco to come trotting along the path. He hadn't, and when Travis came out of the woods, the truck was gone. That's when his stomach got nervous. Rosco never went anywhere without him or Grandpa. And Grandpa never took Rosco anywhere except to the vet.

He went inside and shuffled around the house, looking out windows and waiting. Lunchtime came and went without a phone call. The truck finally pulled up in the driveway late in the afternoon, and Travis ran out to the front porch.

"Where's Rosco?" he asked as Grandpa got out of the truck.

"Not with you?"

"No, I made him stay. He wasn't here when you left?"

"I thought he was with you."

Travis followed Grandpa into the house. Grandpa

cracked a beer and slugged it back, his Adam's apple moving under loose skin as he swallowed.

"That means he's been gone for hours," said Travis. "We'd better go look for him."

Grandpa took another drink, then looked at Travis for the first time.

"He's an old dog, Trav. Old dogs sometimes go away and don't come back."

"What do you mean?" Travis's voice cracked high.

"I mean he might have left for a reason, and we should leave him be."

Travis walked miles through the woods that afternoon, along the roads and fields until after dark. His throat hurt from calling, and his whistle went dry. When he got home, the truck was gone. Maybe Rosco had come back, hurt or sick, and Grandpa had taken him to the vet.

Travis turned on the TV and stared at it, waiting for the sound of truck tires on the gravel. When it finally came, it pulled Travis out of a deep foggy sleep, and early-morning sun filtered in the window. He jumped off the couch and ran out to the porch.

Grandpa got out of the truck, unsteady.

"Where's Rosco?" asked Travis.

"How should I know?"

The words shot liquid-hot rage surging through Travis. Grandpa hadn't been at the vet; he'd gone to the bar. Stayed out all night with Rosco missing, maybe sick or hurt somewhere. Travis stepped forward hard just as Grandpa grabbed the railing. Grandpa flinched, lost his balance, and fell slow-motion off the stair. He landed in a crumple on the gravel.

The hot liquid inside Travis turned immediately to cold sludge, the way it did every time he blew and someone ended up on the ground. Grandpa stared up as if he'd never seen Travis before. Then he shook his head and awkwardly pushed himself off the gravel. He limped back to the truck without a look or a word. He got in, slammed the door, started the engine, and left.

Travis spent hours in the woods again, calling, whistling, looking under bushes. His stomach was a wrench of gut juice, and his mind spun with half-hammered excuses. *I didn't touch you! You fell all by yourself.* And over it all: *He's an old dog, Trav. Old dogs sometimes go away and don't come back.*

The truck was in the drive when he got home.

"Rosco?" he called softly as he opened the screen door.

Grandpa got up from the couch. He looked like he'd been crawling under bushes himself. White-faced, the skin around his jaw sagging. He picked up his keys from the counter, and his hand shook so much, they clanked together. "I'm going out for a bit."

"I didn't find him," said Travis. "Don't you even care?"

Grandpa walked out the door without answering. Travis stared at the refrigerator. Did drinking really make it all go away? As if nothing happened, nothing hurt, and you just don't care? Maybe it was worth a try. He pulled the handle and looked in. Milk, eggs, cheese. A few apples. Not a single can of beer. He checked the liquor cabinet. Completely empty. No wonder Grandpa had to go out.

The house was creepy-quiet. No doggie snores, no click-click of toenails or thump of scratching, no slurping in the water dish. Quiet in a way Travis had never heard, not as far back as he could remember.

Grandpa always said a good dog needs work, and the night Travis's mom went to the hospital and didn't come back, Rosco found his job. Travis's dad died in an accident three months later, and then Rosco forgot all about being anyone's dog. He became Travis's mom and dad and a couple of brothers thrown in. That's what Grandpa said.

For almost a month now, Travis had woken up every day with no Rosco. No mom, no dad, no imaginary brothers. Grandpa had given him up from the first day. He didn't even care. What if Travis disappeared? *Oh, well, sometimes kids go away and don't come back.*

Travis kicked a beer can. It landed with a dull tink on the road ahead, and a roar exploded from the ditch on the other side of a driveway. Travis jumped straight sideways and came down eyeball-to-eyeball with a snarling, mean-eyed dog. Its lip was curled all the way back to show pink-and-black gums above sharp white teeth.

"Ohhhhh, hey, easy now."

Travis backed away, looking down, sideways, anywhere but directly into those eyes. His body twitched with wanting to run. He forced himself to step slow and willed the dog to stay in its driveway. The dog kept snarling that low-throated growl, its tail pointing straight back. One wrong move and it would start throat ripping. Travis kept talking in a low, easy voice.

"Sorry, I didn't see your driveway there. I know, you're just doing your job, and woo, you're good at it. Look, I'm leaving, see? Here I go."

He didn't take a full breath until he was a good fifty feet away. Then he snuck a look over his shoulder. The dog trotted back up the drive, all relaxed, looking like he'd just gone out to get the mail and not like he'd been threatening murder. Travis grinned. He knew how that felt. *KaBLOW,* snarl, and snap, and then it's over, and hey, did I just bite your leg off? Sorry — I didn't really mean to.

A woodpecker hammered nearby, and Travis sucked in a big lungful of crisp air. He stepped into the cornfield, walked down a row far enough that he couldn't see the road, and lay down. The ground under his back was solid, dry, reassuring. The corn enclosed him in green, stalks on either side, the blades forming a shifting ceiling overhead.

Maybe that was his problem. He'd been raised by a dog, so he didn't know how to act right around people. Grandpa was no help — that was for sure. In the days after Rosco left, he was either gone or holed up in his room. After a few days of that, he told Travis that he'd been going to Alcoholics Anonymous. And that they were moving.

"We can't leave! What if Rosco comes back?"

"Trav, it's been almost a week. He's not coming back."

"But what about that dog that took months to get from Texas to Alaska? He might be doing something like that."

"And Rosco got to Texas how?"

After that, everything rattled by in an unreal kind of nightmare. Packing up, cleaning the place where they'd always lived. At first Travis refused to help. What if Rosco came back and they were gone? Grandpa finally called Chuck, the landlord, and asked him to give the new renters their number and keep an eye out for Rosco. He talked at Travis all the time about "one day at a time" and "easy does it" and blahblah. He said over and over that it was high time for things to change.

Well, they'd changed, all right. Travis pushed himself up off the ground. He emerged from the cornfield and looked back toward the snarling dog's driveway. Next time he went by there, he'd have a little bit of something good to eat in his pocket. He turned the other way and kept walking.

Velveeta on SATURDAY

This day started with reality crawling up my face and jabbing me in the eyeballs before I was even awake. Reminding me it's all no-Calvin weekends. Then I remembered: new job.

Connie sent me to the bakery. She uses cookies and doughnut holes to lure people into the library, and then she hits them over the head with books. I told her I don't read books, and she said, "If you work in my library, you do," and I asked her if she was going to fire me and she shoved a book in my hands.

Calvin, your friend Connie is a fanatic.

But she gave me twenty dollars for working and a few doughnut holes, even though I kept running across the street to the Laundromat to punch quarters, because when else am I going to do it? After work, I hid the laundry under a towel and headed home, rattling my little red wagon behind me.

When I got to the hedges on the library side yard, Travis suddenly apparated in front of me. I spun a round kick to his head, dropped to the ground, and swept his feet out from under, all Crouching Tiger and Hidden Dragon. Or maybe I just shoved him really hard in the chest. I'm not sure — I was kinda startled.

I stood over him and said, "Holy crapoly, man, don't jump out at me like that. I just about killed you with my lethal hands."

He stood up smiling, like I couldn't have done him a bigger favor than bashing him flat on the cement. I told him I was going to buy him a cowbell so he couldn't sneak up on me, and he lit up so red, you could find your way through a dark tunnel by the glow off his face. I have to say, it's cute, the way he reds up so fast.

Then he got all nosy, asking what was in my wagon. I told him it was contraband from the crystal-meth lab and pointed at the library. He asked what was in there really. "Um, llllibrrrarrrreeee," I said, pointing to that big sign in front of the building.

Talk about sensitive. He flinched like I'd just smacked him twelve days from Tuesday. He walked off without even saying good-bye. So to make up for being sarcastic, I called after him and offered up a doughnut hole. He turned around and stared at that day-old doughnut hole like I'd offered him rat bait from a garbage can, which kinda ouched my feelings because I was just trying to make up for knocking him over and all.

"Okay, I'm busted," I said. "The doughnut hole is laced with crystal meth. What are you going to do, arrest me here on the sidewalk? Not without a warrant, buddy."

I shoved the bakery bag back in the wagon and started walking. I got about five steps away when he called out my name, so of course I had to turn around.

"I'm not really an undercover cop," he said.

We faced off like gunfighters on Main Street, fifty paces

apart, staring at each other. He stood there, hands in his pockets, looking like he wouldn't know how to shoot even if you handed him a .357 snub with PULL THIS written in pink nail polish on the trigger.

"I'm not really carrying meth," I said. "I'm just taking my laundry home."

He nodded. I nodded. He gave me one of his little shadow smiles and walked off.

Here's the other thing about Travis. He has the prettiest eyes. I'm not sure what color they are. Sometimes I think they're green, but then I think maybe they're brown or even dark blue. I can't get a good look because of how he half shades them with his lids or looks away. Someday I hope to get ten seconds or so to have a good stare and call them a color.

Chapter Six

Monday morning, Travis had just put the toast in when Grandpa's morning hack-and-spit show started. Then came the flick of the lighter, and smoke crawled under the bedroom door.

"Don't suppose you made me any." Grandpa stepped into the kitchen, a cigarette hanging out of the corner of his mouth.

Travis shook his head. He spread butter on his toast.

"Nope, course not," Grandpa answered himself. He closed the bathroom door behind him and followed up with more gross morning noises. The house was too small, with every door opening onto the kitchen/living room area. You could put two of this house, or maybe three, into their old place.

By the time Grandpa came out of the bathroom, Travis was at the sink, washing dishes.

"Why are you up so early, anyway?"

"Felt like it."

"You've turned into a fair smart-ass, you know that? You get all your homework done this weekend, smart boy?"

Travis shut off the water and turned around.

"Since when do you care about my homework?"

"Since I quit drinking. You know how many days I got?"

"Days of what?"

"Days sober, Travis. Do you notice anything besides yourself around here?"

Travis opened the front door and let some air in so he wouldn't pass out from secondhand smoke.

"Thirty days today," said Grandpa. "Thirty days without a drink."

"Congratulations. When you going to quit smoking?"

Grandpa shifted his cigarette to his left hand, made a pistol out of his right, squinted down the barrel of his finger at Travis, and shot. Then he blew his fingertip like he thought he was some old-time cowboy and gave a hard grin.

"Get outta here," he said. "Before you ruin my good day."

Travis had over an hour before school started, so he

grabbed a doughnut and turned right instead of left. He walked fast along the gravel shoulder, trying to warm up. The heavy dew had a whisper of frost, and the sun was high enough to light the treetops but not to put any warmth on the road.

He slowed as he got close to the dog's driveway and gave a high-low whistle. The dog came roaring down the driveway, lip snarled and hair spiking up the back of his neck. Travis stood maybe fifteen feet away from the drive, turned slightly away from the dog. He broke off a chunk of doughnut and tossed it between them. The dog ignored it and stood with legs and tail stiff, *row wow wow*, but his lip wasn't curled quite as high as last time.

"Hi, dog," said Travis. "Whatsamatter, you don't like day-olds?"

He crossed to the other side of the road, keeping up a low, steady stream of chatter.

"You want to be more careful, jumping out at people like that. You could end up on your butt on the sidewalk."

The dog stopped barking, but a growl vibration motored deep in his throat. Travis tossed another chunk to the shoulder on the dog's side of the road. The dog glanced down, then locked his gaze back on Travis.

"I'm leaving, see? Didn't even come close to your drive."

After a few more steps, he turned to walk backward and caught the dog nosing the doughnut up off the ground. Travis smiled. Not so tough after all.

He was tempted to step into the cornfield, but everything was wet with dew and he'd be soaked before he got five feet in. He followed the same route he'd taken Saturday, circling into town. He came up to the place where Velveeta had knocked him flat. He'd seen her coming out of the building and panicked, hiding behind the hedge, but then she'd turned that way and he was afraid she'd see him hiding, so he'd stepped out and *whomp*. Smackdown.

What a complete and total bluefish. No wonder they all made fun of him in Salisbury. If they started in on him here, it'd be even worse, because there was no place to go. Back home, he used to pick up dead branches and whack them on trees as hard as he could, breaking them down to kindling. Or he'd grab the ax and work on the woodpile, slamming into chunks of oak, splitting them clean. With that and Rosco on his side, he could put a cork in it and when the hissing and fssshing started up, just walk away.

Unless someone touched him. Then it was all over. Not Velveeta, though. He grinned and shook his head. She had knocked him flat so fast, he hadn't had time to get mad. She bashed him harder than he'd knocked Joey Nizmanski last November in the boys' bathroom, when Joey hit his head on the sink and got himself a concussion and Travis a suspension.

All Travis got from Velveeta was a bit of road rash on his hands. No name calling, no laughing, not even a halfway eye-rolled glance that said he wasn't worth looking at. No, instead there was the sound of her voice when she said she wasn't carrying meth, just laundry, and the nod that came after. Whatever she'd packed into the words and the nod, it was something Travis had never felt coming his way before. It almost made him look forward to school. He picked up his pace so he wouldn't be late for first period.

Velveeta on MONDAY

I don't get it. I figured Travis and I would be partners for the social-studies project. I had this great idea about a really easy skit we could do, but he kept saying no to everything and then at lunch he went down from six words to two. I couldn't even get him to crack his famous tiny almost-smile.

After our Saturday-morning sidewalk shoot-out, I thought we might actually be friends of some kind.

But what do I know about friends? Everyone loves Velveeta, hahaha. I'm everyone's entertainment monkey, and they all want me to sit with them at lunch or be in their group. But how often do they invite me to their birthday parties?

Remember my ninth birthday? When you got all those goofy stuffed animals from Goodwill and put party hats on them? That was the best birthday of my whole life.

Chapter Seven

Velveeta ignored Travis all day Tuesday. She didn't jab him in the neck one time during social studies, and when Ms. Gordon said they'd be working on projects the next day, she didn't say a word.

He'd figured the social-studies project would ruin everything, but he wasn't ready for it to happen quite so fast. She didn't look over at him during reading. She sat with a bunch of girls at lunch, and he sat alone, with Amber Raleigh at the other end of the table, reading. At least in Salisbury he ate with the other dumb kids, not all by himself.

After school, Travis couldn't bring himself to go back to the empty house. He turned off Main onto a shady side street. A block down, a gravel alley on his right opened into a park. Trees scattered shade over rusty playground equipment, and beyond that, wooden bleachers flanked a baseball diamond behind the Main Street taverns.

He threw his backpack on the grass and sat on an ancient merry-go-round. The surface radiated warmth, and Travis pushed the old metal loose from its rust. The unbalanced weight made it dip-squeak as it went around. He pushed again, and the toe of his white sock, sticking out of the hole in his sneaker, came up brown from the dust. Once he got some motion going, he lay back and watched the green leaves overhead swirl against the deep blue backdrop.

"Hey, Travis."

He sat up sharp. Bradley Whistler stood looking down at him. Travis dragged his foot to brake. Bradley went to the other side of the merry-go-round and kicked a few times to get it going again. The change in weight took out the dip motion, but it still squeaked every time Travis passed the slide.

"Whatcha doing?" asked Bradley.

"Nothing," said Travis.

They squeaked around a few times, and then Bradley said, "So, I was wondering, did you know Velveeta before?"

"No, why?"

"'Cause you two are tight and it's only the second week. She sits by you every day at lunch."

Every day till now. Bradley must not have seen him sitting alone.

"How do you know her?"

"I don't, really," said Travis.

"Sure seems like she likes you."

She only liked him because of Bradley's shoe, and that was over now, anyway. The merry-go-round's squeaks grew louder in the silence, slowed, then ground to a stop. Bradley got off, grabbed the hand bars, pushed a few steps to get it going again, and jumped back on.

"People say a lot of stuff about her," he said.

"Like what?"

"Lots of stuff. Like she gets drunk every night and her brother's a drug dealer. And she does the wild thing with older guys. I don't think it's all true, though."

Travis dug his heel into the dust and stopped the circling. He shifted sideways to look at Bradley.

"If you don't think it's true, why are you saying it?"

Bradley blinked and cocked his head.

"Hm. Why did I say it? Roger roger, that's a really good question."

He looked down at his feet for a long moment, then back up at Travis.

"You know how sometimes you don't know something is stupid until it falls out of your mouth and then it's too late?"

Travis didn't have an answer for that one, since he

usually kept his stupid thoughts in his own head. He pushed with his foot to get the squeak going again.

"I think Velveeta is smart," said Bradley. "I used to think she was dumb."

"Why'd you think that?"

"She wore the same clothes all the time and got in fights and stuff. You know how that can make someone seem dumb. So, are you going out with her?"

"No."

"Not doing the wild thing?"

Travis shot Bradley a look.

"Kidding," said Bradley, putting his hands up. "Sorry."

"I gotta go." Travis dragged his foot to stop the spin. Bradley was starting to make him twitchy, and he didn't need a twitch right now. "Later, Brad."

"Bradley."

"Okay, Bradley," said Travis.

He picked up his backpack and started walking. Bradley followed him.

"I'm sorry. That wasn't funny, about you and Velveeta and the wild thing. I meant it to be funny. I like Velveeta, but I'm kind of scared of her. I've never talked to her."

"Never?"

"Well, sometimes when we're in a group or something, but that's all. I think of her as having a sword in her mouth that she whips out and chops you up with before you can even figure out what's going on. So really, you're not going out? You're just friends?"

"We're not going out." Travis said it harder, with an edge.

"How did you get to be friends? I've never been friends with a girl."

They cut between the buildings to Main Street. Bradley either didn't notice that Travis was edgy or he didn't care. He kept right on like they were buddies, like they talked about girls and friends all the time.

"I turn here," he said when they got to Water Street. "See you tomorrow?"

No smoking guys on the picnic table, so Travis leaned on the bridge railing and watched Bradley walk along Water Street. He'd really been dumb enough to think Velveeta might be his friend. That lasted just long enough to hurt when it was gone. Now he was down to nothing, unless you counted Bradley.

Travis half wished the picnic-table guys would come up behind him. Wished they'd start something, and then he could blow loose all over them and whatever happened, it wouldn't be his fault.

The next morning, Travis turned from his locker between first and second bell and slammed into Chad Cormick.

"Watch it, Roberts," said Cormick.

Travis's breath stopped in his throat. Cormick shifted in front of him, blocking his way. Travis's shoulders crawled up around his neck, and his hands twitched toward fists.

"How's your hoop?" Cormick asked.

"My what?"

Cormick balanced an imaginary basketball overhead with his right hand, bent his knees, and delivered the ball, jumping high and flicking his wrist. He watched his shot, his hand still hanging in the air, and then shook his head.

"Air ball." He turned to Travis. "Hoop. Do you?"

"Not really." Travis's heart still hammered, but his back relaxed and his shoulders eased down.

"Time to start," said Chad. "This school has a height problem, did you notice? We went one and nine last year. We practice in the gym at lunch. You and me and the shorties — maybe we can go at least fifty-fifty."

"I suck." Travis moved to go around Cormick.

"Tall suck beats short suck." Cormick sidestepped in front of him. "Maybe you need a little practice."

Just as Travis started to feel crowded, Cormick hopped back, grinning, and dribbled his air ball on the floor between them, practically begging Travis to reach out and make the steal. When he didn't move, Chad juked left and ran down the hall, still dribbling.

Travis moved along on the wave of kids to first period. Relief rivered down his neck and through his shoulders. A fight in the hallway said bluefish almost as clear as tripping over every word when you read out loud. He sat in front of Velveeta's empty seat. She came in the door just as the last bell rang.

"I see Chad tried to seduce you with his basketball dreams," she said as she slid into her chair.

Travis turned, surprised she was talking to him. She grinned and wiggled her eyebrows.

"Velveeta sees all. He asked me yesterday if you played, so I knew he'd be on you about it. You're the only guy in the class taller than him."

"Tall doesn't mean good."

"We need some tall here. Have you noticed how short all the guys are?" she said. "It's something in the water. Just watch: Cormick only drinks bottled. So you're not going to start basketballing at lunch?"

"No, I don't like basketball."

"I like you more all the time. I know you were pining for me at lunch yesterday, so today I will once again grace you with my Velveetic presence."

She flipped her scarf dramatically over her face and batted her eyelashes at him. He faced front quickly so she wouldn't see the big smile breaking across his face.

"Okay, settle down," called Ms. Gordon. "Tomorrow, we're going to take the whole class period to work on your projects, so make sure you have everything you need for that. Presentations start Monday."

"Did you read your part yet?" Velveeta asked.

Travis shook his head. Velveeta tapped her pencil on the tip of his ear.

"Get on it," she whispered.

Velveeta on WEDNESDAY

I decided why I like Travis. It's not just the pretty eyes. It's everything he doesn't say. I sat with Becca and Megan and Cassidy yesterday, and their mouths gushed like fire hydrants spray-blasting me the whole time. They talked about Travis and said he's cute but dumb and boring, and they waited for me to agree but I did not. I said nothing for once. So then they talked about everybody else in the whole school. You want to talk about boring — THAT was boring.

Okay, I know, I spray more words out than anybody — I KNOW that. But at least I'm not boring. Not to me, anyway. Maybe nobody is boring to themselves, but we all bore the heck out of each other.

Except Travis. He doesn't bore me at all. I like how his eyes are full of words but mostly he doesn't let them out of his mouth except for a zinger here or there like, "I like your scarf." I know he's not an undercover cop, but I still think he has a secret. Nobody shuts up that much unless they have a secret. He gave me his whole dessert today. It was only canned peaches, but still.

Hey, I know. I bet he's secretly tragically dying of leukemia. That's why he switched schools. He wants to be brave till the end, and not have anybody know.

But as I was getting up to leave, there was McQueen with his supersonic eyes, staring at us. I bet he knows about Travis's leukemia.

Chapter Eight

Travis peeled his eyelids open and pulled the towel back to look out the window. Cold gray rain. Plus it was Thursday, social-studies project day. He closed his eyes again.

"You up yet?" Grandpa yelled.

Travis gave out something between a grunt and a groan.

"What's wrong with you?" Grandpa asked, opening the door.

"I'm sick." The dread in his stomach could easily work its way up to the flu or maybe food poisoning.

"You going to ralph?"

"Maybe. Probably."

"Okay. I'll call in to work so I can stay here and babysit you."

Grandpa turned back to the kitchen, but he left the door open so Travis could see him at the sink, looking out the window and smoking. The smell and the gray and the closing-in walls of the house made Travis think he really might ralph.

"I thought you couldn't miss work to babysit me."

"If you're sick, I'm staying home." Grandpa said it without turning around.

"Since when?" muttered Travis as he got out of bed.

"Feeling better?" asked Grandpa when Travis got out of the shower.

"Yup."

"Thought so." Grandpa said it with a grin and a cackle.

The social-studies class spread out around the room in pairs. Velveeta pulled Travis into the back corner, and they sat on the floor. She opened her textbook.

"So, look," said Velveeta. "I still think this Paleolith-Neolith skit is the way to go. We turn this page into a script, and it'll be funny. Me Paleo, you Jane. Ha, ha, ha."

"I thought homework was against your religion," said Travis.

"What homework? Who's home? I'm not home — are you home?"

"I don't really like skits."

"You'd rather hold up a boring poster and point at it?"

"I'd rather do neither." If he kept saying no to everything, maybe she'd give up.

"Look, Travattini. If we gotta get up there, we might as well not be boring. You want to be Neo, then?"

"No."

"You've got a better idea? Cough it up."

"How are you two doing?" Ms. Gordon knelt down next to them.

"Great," said Velveeta. "We're comparing notes on our reading here."

"Okay, good. Let me know if you need help."

"So what do you want to do?" asked Velveeta as Ms. Gordon moved on to the next pair.

"I'm not doing anything," Travis dropped his voice. "You should get a different partner."

"Why? I'm not good enough to be your partner, or what?"

"I'm not doing the project. Do it without me."

"Okay, me neither." Velveeta slammed her textbook shut. "No homework means no projects."

She drew a tic-tac-toe grid, and they played until the bell rang.

Travis tried to give Velveeta his chocolate pudding at lunch. He handed her the entire bowl, but she pushed it back.

"You have to keep your strength up," she said. "It'll slide down easy."

"Keep my strength up for what?"

"*You* know."

Her dishes were already scraped clean. She leaned forward on her elbows and stared at him. Her eyes knocked on his brain, trying to see things he'd rather keep hidden.

"So if you and Bradley aren't friends," he said, looking for a distraction, "why do you care that I gave his shoe back?"

Velveeta grinned like he'd just crowned her queen.

"A question! A complete direct question, just for me. You must really like me after all."

"So why do you?"

"How do you know we're not friends?"

"He told me."

"What did he do, just walk up to you in the hall and say, 'Hey, I am not friends with the Great and Powerful Velveeta'?"

"No." Travis finished off the pudding. "We hung out in the park the other day."

"Hung out? You and Bradley Whistler? Very fascinating."

"So why do you care about his shoe?"

"I don't. It was the way you did it. There it is, first day of school, like always, somebody stealing Whistler's stuff, him doing the hoppy no-shoe dance."

She stood up and imitated Bradley's shuffle-step.

"But then! Mr. Stealth comes rockin' onto the scene" — she took a few steps back and then slid up in a smooth saunter — "and delivers the shoe without one word, all incognito." She passed a pretend shoe behind her back and flipped it to a pretend Bradley. "Then melts into the crowd like Bradley's own personal secret superhero. That was a class act."

Travis shrugged and looked down at the table. His face burned. Was it red? Could she tell?

The bell rang, and he picked up his tray and followed Velveeta to the garbage can. What would she say if she knew what Bradley had asked, about them doing the wild thing? If she liked complete direct questions so much, she'd love that one.

As Travis turned toward the hallway, he glanced at the teachers' table. McQueen was staring right at him and Velveeta. When he caught Travis's eye, he smiled. Like he knew something.

Velveeta on THURSDAY

After the last bell, Ms. Gordon snagged me and asked why we hadn't turned in a project outline. She made sad eyes and said things about our futures. Not that I have a future, but Travis probably does, so I went by his locker and tried to guilt him on board by saying I'd flunk if he wouldn't be my partner. He said I should ask Bradley Whistler if I needed a partner so bad.

I think that was a tiny bit mean. Bradley Whistler would never be my partner, even if I begged him, which I won't, but that's not even the point. The point is, Travis sounded all mad when he said it and started walking really fast, like he was trying to ditch me. So I grabbed him by the arm, which was a mistake, because he yanked away like I had cootie slime all over my fingers.

He said (I still can't believe this), "Quit bugging me. I'm not doing it."

"Bugging you?" I said, and I sidestepped in front of him because, I don't know, I'm stupid. He looked at me like I was the evil enemy, shoulder-banged by, and boom-kabang, off he went — didn't even look back.

This does not fit with anything about Travis. What's going on? This whole time I've been thinking he likes me a little bit, maybe more than just ha-ha funny Velveeta to entertain him through his leukemia. But have I actually been bugging him?

Chapter Nine

Travis steamed through town. His face didn't cool off until he was almost to the bridge. Everyone should just leave him alone, and that included Velveeta.

The guys sat on the picnic table. Their eyes crawled on him from way off.

"Hey, kid, what's your name?" one of them called as he came up close.

He stalked across the bridge. Why didn't they just do whatever they were going to do? Enough with sitting around yelling stuff.

"Hey, skinny boy, did you hear my man Chilson? He asked your name. You're not being very polite."

Travis turned and stared at Chilson, the blond guy. Chilson showed his teeth in a fake smile.

"What's the matter, too scared to talk?" asked the one with long dark hair.

Travis shook his head and waited, giving them a chance to start it. Chilson flicked a butt in his direction and then turned away. Travis's shoulders went down. He let out a slow breath. Not today. Maybe some other day.

At dinner, Grandpa passed him some bright-orange mac and cheese out of a box, with frozen peas tossed in, and said, "I've been thinking. You should go out for a sport or get a job."

"Why?" Travis poked his fork in and came up with a drippy straw stack.

"You need something to do."

"I had plenty to do at the old place."

"Good cold Christ, boy, how long you going to keep chewing that song? Can we just try and live in the present here? Maybe for one day?"

Travis didn't answer. He scooped up more orange watery macaroni. Grandpa leaned across the table and poked Travis's shoulder with a sharp finger.

"You answer when I talk to you, boy."

Travis glared at him.

"Trying to kill me with that look? Trav, I'm trying

here, in case you didn't notice. You think you could climb on board even for a minute?"

Travis scraped his chair back and took his plate to the sink. When he turned around, Grandpa had gotten to his feet.

"You wanna take a poke at me?" Grandpa stepped closer. He tapped his white-stubbly, saggy-skinned jaw. "Think that might make you feel better?"

The smell of tobacco and aftershave rolled off him. Travis clamped his fists in his pockets and stepped sideways, against the counter.

"Just leave me alone."

"No." Grandpa said it soft as he reached out and tapped Travis on the chest with his bony finger. "I won't."

Velveeta on FRIDAY

I'm not going to school today. Travis is too good to do my brilliant skit idea, fine. Let him figure it out for himself. I am spending my day here in your trailer.

The madre was actually up this morning, which made it more fun to act like I was rushing off to school. She announced that she's done drinking forever, which, you know, means she's going to act like she gives a crap for a day or two. She said she's going shopping to buy some chicken and potatoes and make a big dinner. I said that's great, Ma. I'll be hungry after my long day of learning.

Bad part: she called Buttface Jimmy to ask him over for dinner. Good part: he didn't answer.

Chapter Ten

The bell rang for social studies. The classroom door closed. The seat behind Travis was empty. No whispers, no pencil jab. When they broke off to work on their projects, Travis doodled in the margins of notebook paper.

"Is your outline ready to go, Travis?" Ms. Gordon knelt next to his desk.

He shook his head.

"Did you and Velveeta decide what you're doing?"

"We're not partners."

"So—you're going to work individually?" she asked, and Travis nodded. "You'll still need to turn in an outline by the end of class today."

When the bell rang, Travis was the first one out the door.

Fourth period, Travis stared at the line drawings in the fox book as the minutes ticked by.

"Travis Roberts," McQueen called. Travis's head jerked up like it was on a string. "Come into my office, please. Bring your book. I'd like to cut into your lunch period for a minute or two."

Travis took a deep breath. First the project, now this. Skate-by time was over.

"Have a good weekend, people," McQueen said as the bell rang. "I know you'll all spend it reading."

He turned to Travis.

"How's the book going?"

"Fine."

"You didn't turn in the paragraph on literature last week. And you turned in a blank paper for the vocabulary quiz on Wednesday."

Travis slid into his teacher-talk slouch. He stopped hearing the words. McQueen's voice was a low and distant rumble, like a summer storm that passed north, never coming close.

BAM!

The crash lifted Travis all the way out of his chair.

"Sorry," McQueen said, grinning. "But not really. I wanted your attention, and the book bang does it every time. Are you here with me now?"

Travis nodded. His heart skipped as if McQueen had just shot a lightning jolt straight into his chest.

"What I asked was, do you want to?"

"Want to what?"

McQueen didn't take his eyes off Travis's for a second. His voice went quiet, nighttime quiet.

"Learn to read, Mr. Roberts. Do you want to learn to read?"

Travis swallowed hard as the heat crawled up his face.

"I can read." His voice didn't sound like his own.

"Do you want to learn to read better? Read easily? Without so much struggle?"

McQueen's voice was a low-running motor, and his eyes were soft behind the glasses.

"You, Travis Roberts, can learn to read. But only if you, Travis Roberts, decide to learn. If you decide, I'll teach you, and you will learn."

A clump of mud rose in Travis's throat and stuck there. He couldn't have said anything if he wanted to. His eyes pricked.

"When you decide, let me know," said McQueen. "Now, go to lunch."

Travis went into a stall in the boys' room, closed the door, and sat on the toilet. The mud clump stuck in his throat, not going up or down.

Mrs. Keatley, the reading specialist at Salisbury, used to say, "Try, Travis. Can't you just try?" At first he'd tried really hard. After a while, Mrs. Keatley's lipsticky lips got less smiley when she saw him, and they both knew it was a waste of time. He stopped trying.

He couldn't read. Not really. Not like Velveeta, or Amber, or Chad or Bradley or Megan or everyone else. Even Grandpa could read. He swallowed hard, pushing the mud down. Maybe he should try again. *Just try, Travis.*

The memory of Mrs. Keatley's voice was enough to stop him. He stood up, slung his backpack over his shoulder, and rubbed his hands hard over his face. He stepped out of the stall just as Bradley came in from the hallway.

"Hey, Travis, where's Velveeta?" he asked. "Is she sick?"

"How would I know?"

"Do you know about the girls' report cards?" Bradley held out a piece of paper.

Travis scanned the paper and found his name. Across from it was a line of letters. A couple of As, a B and a C and two Fs. Of course there were Fs.

"They've been doing report cards on all of us, and Cassidy made me a copy. I flunked tall and hot, but I got a C for cute and an A for smart. I don't get how hot and cute are different, do you?"

Travis shook his head and handed the paper back to Bradley. He couldn't even tell what he got the two As for.

"Chad was the only one who got an A for funny."

A couple more guys banged in, and Travis headed for

the lunchroom. He got tomato soup, figuring that could slide past the mud clump without too much trouble. He sat in the usual spot by himself. Amber Raleigh sat at the end of the table, reading.

Travis glanced over as she turned another page. He reached in his backpack, took out the fox book, and looked at the picture. Remembered the beginning of the story McQueen had read. He traced the fox with his finger and looked at the hound in the background.

He opened to the first page. It. Was. A. Something, so, something, that, something, the . . .

He didn't want to try. Just the idea of trying made his guts clench. But McQueen hadn't said, "Try." He'd said, "I will teach you and you will learn." Like it was a done deal. Like he knew.

After the last bell, Travis stood in the doorway of McQueen's classroom. McQueen was there. Travis almost backed out. Then he took a deep breath, walked quickly across the room, and stopped in the doorway of the office.

McQueen looked up from the book he was reading.

"Yes, Mr. Roberts?"

"I decided."

"Decided what, Mr. Roberts?"

"I want to learn."

McQueen grinned like he'd been waiting all day for Travis to stand in his doorway and say just exactly that.

"I'll see you here Monday morning at eight. That'll give us half an hour before the first bell. Bring *Haunt Fox* with you."

"Okay," said Travis, backing away.

"Travis," said McQueen, "have a good weekend."

Velveeta on SATURDAY

The madre made roasted chicken last night, and mashed potatoes and even some carrots and a frozen cherry pie, unfrozen. Then we played cribbage for a couple of hours. It was very down-home and fun. I won three dollars off her, so add that to my library stash and I'm officially rich.

Jimmy never showed. Maybe he got arrested or took too many drugs and he's dead in his crappy apartment and I'll never have to see him again. If I were my brother's keeper, I'd make him wear a muzzle like Hannibal Lecter in *Silence of the Lambs*.

I called the electric company and told them to turn on the power in your trailer. Easy. I just used the madre's info and told them to send the bill here. I asked Connie at work today if she would write a check to the electric company if I give her cash for it. I told her my mom won't pay the electric bill and I have to. That was supposed to make her feel sorry for me. I think it worked. She said she would, anyway.

Yesterday was a really long day. I wonder if Travis missed me. Probably he feels bad now for saying I was bugging him. Or maybe he's just happy I wasn't there bugging him. Maybe I should just stay here in this trailer and never come out.

At first, I was a little scared to be in here because I thought you might be ghosting around, but you're definitely not. I've looked everywhere, even under the bed.

There's nothing in here but empty.

CHAPTER ELEVEN

"Mr. Roberts!" McQueen waved Travis into his office. "You made my day just by showing. Did you bring the — oh, good, you brought it. Here, give it to me, take a seat."

McQueen opened the fox book, paged ahead, and started reading. Travis stared at him, his heart pounding in his throat.

"Wait," he said.

McQueen paused and looked up, his eyebrows raised.

"I thought you were going to teach me to read."

"I am."

"But you're just reading to me."

"I thought you liked this story."

"I do, but..."

"Are you a teacher, Travis?"

Travis shook his head no.

"Have you been able to teach yourself to read?"

Again, no.

"Okay, then, you're just going to have to trust me on this. You want to learn; I want to teach. Sit back and relax. Listen to every word. No spacing out."

McQueen's voice took Travis back to the swamp, and slowly his heart settled down. The fox got jumped by a wildcat in the swamp and got away. A blizzard raged around him and he caught a whiff of chickens from a nearby farm, and the first bell rang and McQueen stopped reading.

"So? Do you still like it?"

Travis nodded.

"Me too. We're on page twelve." He handed the book across the desk. "When you come to reading, bring this and a pencil. Start on page one, and circle every word you don't know."

"But I'll mess up your book."

"Can I give you six oceans of how much I don't care about a few marks in that book?" said McQueen. "But use a pencil, not a pen."

"So, I circle every word I don't know?"

"That's right, every one. I'm here Mondays, Wednesdays, and Fridays before school. Come early any of those days. The more often you come, the faster you'll learn. Go on, now, or you'll be late for first period."

Travis wove his way through the noisy hall. What if it could really work? Mrs. Keatley never told him to circle words. Maybe McQueen knew what he was doing. Velveeta was already in her seat in Ms. Gordon's room.

"A smile!" she said, throwing her arms wide. "With teeth! Does that mean I'm not bugging you too much right now?"

"Where were you Friday?" He turned sideways in his seat.

"I took a little Velveeta time. Did you miss me?"

"Yes."

"And you're sorry for saying I was bugging you?"

Travis tried to decide if he was or not. He wanted her to quit bugging him about the project, but not about anything else.

"Okay, okay," she whispered. "Don't waste a word on it. Just nod your head yes and you'll be forgiven."

He dipped his head.

"That'll do for now. I'm going to do my brilliant skit without you, unless you beg me to let you in."

Ms. Gordon started class — a full period of presentations. Neither Travis nor Velveeta got called to go. Kids pointed at posters they'd made and droned on about time lines. Velveeta poked Travis in the back of the neck after each one and said, "See? *Boring.*"

Travis didn't pay any attention to the presentations,

though. His fingers itched to open the fox book and circle words. *I can do that,* he told the unsmiley Mrs. Keatley in his mind. *I can do it exactly right.*

Travis carried the book with him all morning, until he finally got to fourth period. He opened to the first page, pulled the book close, and covered it with his hand so nobody could see what he was doing. Just to be fair, he circled the word *chapter,* even though he knew it said *chapter,* because if it wasn't at the top of the page, he wouldn't have known. He closed his eyes to see if he could bring back McQueen's voice reading the chapter title and match it to the print on the page. Started with *R. Rrrrr.* He tried to make the word something he knew.

"Just circle the words." McQueen came up behind Travis, with a hand on his shoulder and a whisper in his ear. "Don't try to figure them out. Just circle."

Travis circled the *R* word. He went on to sneak forty-one circles on that page, dipping his pencil in for a quick mark and then acting like he just happened to be holding it while he read. He'd circled another eleven on the next page by the time the bell rang for lunch.

He sat down across from Velveeta, and she slammed a thick book shut.

"Whew! Nick of time, Travicus. You saved me from this crazy book. McQueen said I have to get up to page one hundred by Monday or he'll flunk me. I think that's blackmail, or maybe it's extortion. Either way I'm sure it's not legal, and besides, this is sicko — it's all about death. Hey, what's with Whistle-Stop?"

Bradley Whistler stood about ten steps away, staring at them.

"Whistle-Stop, what are you looking at?" yelled Velveeta.

Bradley scuttled over and stood behind Travis.

"Can I eat lunch with you?"

"Why for, Mr. Whistler?" asked Velveeta. "You doing some kind of study on the lower classes?"

"Never mind."

"Nonononono, wait!" Velveeta waved her hands. "Relax. Sit down. You're just worried about Travis there, aren't you? He thinks you're cute — he told me so — but don't worry, I'll keep him off you."

"Lying," said Travis out of the side of his mouth as Bradley sat next to him.

"I know," said Bradley.

"Open that pretty purple lunch box," said Velveeta. "Let's see what you've got to share."

Bradley tore loose the Velcro on his purple soft-sided box and pulled out a Tupperware container.

"What's that?" asked Velveeta.

He popped the lid and showed them a mix of pasta, dark-green leaves, and orange chunks.

"It's something my mom makes. It's got spinach and squash and pine nuts. It's good. You want some?"

"Are you kidding?" said Velveeta, holding out her plate. "Of course I do."

Bradley turned to Travis, who shook his head. He'd rather stick with his safe mashed potatoes and chicken.

"My God, Bradley," said Velveeta after her first bite. "Do they feed you like this every day? No wonder you always look so healthy and bright-eyed. Why are you sitting with us? Are you here to tutor us in math?"

"No, I just thought I'd, you know, sit by you."

"I never told you this, Bradley, but you know who you remind me of? Haley Joel Osment, the 'I see dead people' kid from *The Sixth Sense*. Have either of you seen it?"

Travis and Bradley both shook their heads.

"Wasteland," said Velveeta to the ceiling. "I could have been born anywhere in the world, and I live someplace where nobody knows Shyamalan."

"Who's that?" asked Bradley.

"M. Night Shyamalan. He's a writer and director. He's done a bunch of movies. *Sixth Sense* is my favorite, but I also like *Wide Awake* because you can see how he was trying out ideas in that and then he tweaked them around for popular appeal, and bingo, *Sixth Sense*, a blockbuster!"

"How do you know all that?" asked Travis.

"I don't know — it's what I know. We all have something we know. Except for Bradley there. He's Smarty McSmarty-Pants — he knows everything we know and everything else, too."

"No, I don't," said Bradley. "I don't know anything about M. Night Shyama-whatever-you-said. I watch plenty of movies, but I don't pay attention to who wrote or directed them. Someone must have taught you about that."

Velveeta raised her eyebrows as high as they'd go.

"Wow, Bradley. That is very insightful. Maybe you should be a therrrrrrr-a-pist."

The bell rang, and Bradley scooped up the last of his lunch.

"Sit with us again, Bradley," said Velveeta. "Bring us more of your fancy food. It'll be fun."

Bradley looked at Travis like he was in charge.

Travis shrugged and said, "Sure, why not?"

Velveeta on MONDAY

Okay, so Bradley and I have been in school together since kindergarten, and that's the first time he's ever talked to me on purpose. I had to show off and bring up Shyamalan. I wanted him to know I'm not a total idiot. Why do I care? I guess because I think he's kinda fascinating. Besides being off-the-charts smart, he's (a) the only black kid in our class, (b) an unbelievable dork, (c) the shortest of the shorties, (d) really bad at sports, and (e) still alive.

Not only still alive, but not squished. Last year Chad and Mike sat him on the water fountain. If anyone did that to me, I'd leave for the day, but Bradley walked around with wet pants and explained over and over that it was drinking fountain water, not pee. Honestly, I don't know how he survives. Must be the spinach and pine nuts.

Maybe if I got fed that kind of food every day, I'd be more like Bradley. Maybe I'd do my homework and get smart instead of using my science notebook to write to a dead guy.

Chapter Twelve

Travis sat at the card table in his bedroom and circled words. Grandpa had banged out the door for his AA meeting at six thirty, so the house was quiet and the TV off. Travis wanted to have the whole first chapter circled by the time he met with McQueen on Wednesday. He worked at it until his eyes blurred and he accidentally circled words he knew.

Finally, he closed the book, flopped on the couch, and clicked the remote. The truck pulled into the drive. Footsteps tromped on the porch, and the front door opened.

"Look what I got," Grandpa said. "It's to celebrate my thirty days."

Travis twisted to see. Grandpa held up a chunk of sheet cake with white frosting and blue writing. Travis turned back to the TV. He was sick of sweets. Grandpa brought day-olds home from the bakery every day. How much of that stuff could a person eat?

"I thought that was last week," he said.

He glanced up and ran into the squinty-eyeball stare.

"What?"

Grandpa set the cake on the coffee table, grabbed the remote, and turned off the TV.

"Hey, I was watching that!"

"Yeah, that Viagra ad is just full of information you need. Listen, boy, I think you need to start talking. In AA they say if you don't talk about what's chewing on you, it'll eat your guts out."

"I'm not in AA."

"Keep this up and you might be. If your dad would've—"

"Would've what?" Travis sat up.

Grandpa stared at the smoke coming off the end of his cigarette.

"Said something. Maybe he'd be here now, and you could hate him instead of me."

"Said something about what?"

"Travis, he was drunk when he drove into that tree."

"Duh." Even a stupid bluefish had that one figured out a long time ago.

"I'm just saying. Maybe if you talked up, you won't have to be like him or me."

"Nobody likes a chatterbox, remember?" Travis fired the words hard.

Grandpa looked down and ran a hand over his mouth. Loose skin sagged around his Adam's apple. When he finally spoke, his voice was low. Not the crusty-cheery "now that I'm sober" voice.

"I said that a time or two, huh?"

"Try a million."

"Okay, so you're right." Grandpa stubbed out his cigarette. "I'm a shitty bad parent. Was then, am now. Does that help?"

He got up slowly, as if it hurt, and took the cake back to the kitchen. He washed the dishes, opened and closed drawers. Every sound scraped on Travis's nerves. He turned the TV back on. *Does that help?* kept circling around his head. No, it didn't help. The only thing that would help was Rosco. He'd put his warm, heavy head on Travis's lap, and slobber on his leg, and Travis could bury his nose in those silky ears.

Grandpa took the trash out and was gone awhile. When he came back, he closed the door gently behind him.

"You know what we could use?" he said. "A bonfire out in the swamp. Remember how we used to do that when you were a little guy?"

"There's no swamp here." Travis meant to spit the words sharp, but his voice shook.

Grandpa came back over and looked behind the recliner. He creaked down onto his hands and knees and peered under the couch. He put his hands on the coffee table and pushed himself back up, falling onto the couch beside Travis.

"Nope, you're right. I've looked everywhere. No swamp. What are we going to do about that?"

"That's what I'd like to know." Travis got up quickly. As he closed his bedroom door behind him, he barely heard Grandpa's voice.

"Me too, buddy boy," he said. "Me too."

The next morning in social studies, Ms. Gordon called on Velveeta first. She taped a big red P and a big blue N on the board and performed a conversation between the Paleolithic guy and the Neolithic guy, standing first under the P and then under the N.

She compared and contrasted, she rattled off facts about the people from each period, and she had everyone rolling in the aisles. No possible way Travis could have been part of that. He would have ruined it, even if he could have learned the lines.

Velveeta nodded to a standing ovation. She bowed in every direction and waved the end of her blue-on-light-blue scarf. The rest of the presentations were worse than the ones the day before. Travis would have fallen asleep if Velveeta hadn't kept popping bits of commentary in his ear.

When the bell finally rang, they walked out together.

"See, Travail?" she said. "You could've been part of Team Velveeta and shared the glory. You wouldn't even have had to say anything. I would have made you a sign to hold up. You would've been adorable, especially if you would've costumed up in caveman fur."

Chad Cormick jostled hard on the other side of Travis, knocking his books to the floor.

"So, Roberts, is this why you're not hoopin'? Too busy getting some Velveeta on the side?"

The bump and the words lit Travis up before he could douse the flame. He shoved Cormick hard against the lockers.

"Whoa, whoa, easy," said Chad, holding up both hands. "Sorry, sorry, dude, back down. Just a joke."

Travis dropped his hands and stepped back, breathing hard. Reeling it in, clamping down. Motion in the hallway stopped, and a circle of staring eyes surrounded him. Travis stepped backward, out of the center.

"Joke, man, just a joke." Cormick waved his hand back and forth, erasing the whole thing.

"Sorry," said Travis.

He bent down to pick up the books he'd dropped, eyes locked to the floor. In fourth grade on the bus he'd turned on Clay Rosen like that when Clay fsshed him and put gum in his hair. One minute Travis was sitting there, ignoring it all. The next, Clay was holding his nose and crying while blood puddled on the floor of the bus and a whole ring of kids stared at Travis.

Velveeta's dirty black-and-white checkered sneakers appeared next to his pencil. Travis reached for it and tucked it into the spiral of his notebook. When he finally stood up, everyone but Velveeta was gone.

"That was very Fight Clubby of you," she said. "Beating little Chaddy up right here in the school hallway."

"I didn't beat him up."

"It was so manly, defending my honor and all. If I give you a list, will you beat up everyone on it?"

She grinned, big joke. She didn't know about the puddle of blood, or Joey Nizmanski's concussion, or Grandpa in the gravel.

"No." The bell rang for second period.

"Oooh, late for class. What other excitement can happen today?" Velveeta backed away. "See you at lunch."

Travis walked the empty hall to science, still thinking about that fourth-grade day on the bus. Clay's big brother, Marshall, had grabbed Travis by the collar to pull him off, and Travis tore into Marsh so hard that he let go with a shove. "This kid's gone crazy back here," he'd yelled to the bus driver.

After that day, kids still fssh-hissed at him, but mostly they did it from a distance.

When Travis walked into science, he felt eyes on him as he took his seat on the far side of the classroom. He wished Velveeta's eyes were there. Somehow, she saw him differently from everyone else.

Velveeta on a Stupid TUESDAY

The madre made real food again, and this time the butt showed and brought fancy beer from the brewery and they drank their dinner while I ate mine. All he has to do is show up with a bottle and her whole "I'm going to get my head straight and do things right" is gone out the window again. Ha, ha, have a beer, Velveeta. No, thank you, Mother, but gee, thanks for including me, because I can't wait to grow up and be like my big brother.

I can't understand how Jimmy can be so ugly. He seriously has the ugliest face in the world, and when I look in the mirror and try to see how him and me are related, I can see it just around the edges of my ugliness. Calvin, nobody but you understands exactly how much I hate him to hellfire. I wish he'd explode into ashes and never poke his buttface into my life again.

What if Travis really could beat him up? I can see that fight scene on the big screen. Travis would step out from the alley next to the bar and say, "Hey, aren't you Jimmy the butt?" Then, kablow, kablam, slam in the street. Oh my God, can you just see it? Beautiful.

But that would mean mixing Travis with Trailer World. No. That can never happen. Nevernever. Every time I put on a scarf and walk to the end of Pauly Road, I turn into Velveeta, and she might not be much, but she's better than Vida Wojciehowski. And you know what? You brought this

Velveeta version to life. Without you, I'd have a flask of bourbon in my school locker, and I'd be selling drugs and jacking cars and mugging little old ladies and other things I don't even want to think about.

What would I do if I didn't have this place? Right now, I would be wandering around outside in the dark. Instead, I'm tucked away safe here in your electricity-working trailer with the double-bolted door, wrapped up in scarves and watching *Labyrinth*.

Maybe I can move in here. Do you think the madre would even notice?

Chapter Thirteen

Wednesday morning, Travis arrived at McQueen's doorway at 7:45 and sat in the hall outside. He opened the fox book and looked over his hundreds of circled words. Maybe McQueen had no idea how bad it was—maybe he'd thought it would just be ten words a page or so. Anyone could learn that. But this—nobody could learn this many.

"Something wrong, Mr. Roberts?"

McQueen jingled keys out of his pocket and opened the door.

"I circled a lot of words," said Travis.

"Perfect," said McQueen, waving him in. "Let's see what we've got."

"I mean, I didn't know hardly any of those words."

"I know," said McQueen. He held out his hand. "It's a hard book. Let's see."

"Maybe I should have started with an easier book."

"Why?" McQueen flipped through the first few pages. "Are you bored with the story?"

"It's not that. I'm just saying it might be too hard."

"Who's the teacher?"

"You."

"Student?"

"Me."

"You've done excellent work. Top-notch. Now sit back and listen."

McQueen read, his voice like the low hum of a bullfrog on a summer day. The sound and the words eased over Travis, taking him out of the room, out of the walls, into the woods. He closed his eyes and followed the fox through the underbrush until McQueen stopped.

"That's it for today," he said. "But I have a new assignment for you."

He picked up a pen and wrote on a scrap of paper, glancing at the first few pages of *Haunt Fox* as he wrote.

"Look at these words." He handed the paper to Travis.

Five words in a list. Travis didn't know any of them.

"Young." McQueen pointed at the first one. "Say it."

They went over each word together. *Young, night, summer, hunt, branches.* They did the list forward and then backward, McQueen pointing and Travis repeating until he could do them all without a hitch.

"Nice job," said McQueen.

"But that's not reading. I just memorized them."

"Right. We call that word recognition. Keep them with you all day. Write them on your hand with your finger. Link the look and the sound and the feel together. Make friends with them. Once you absolutely know them for sure, anytime, anywhere, then go through the first chapter and use your eraser to uncircle them."

"But I circled like five hundred words. It'll take me years to learn them five words at a time."

"Teacher?" McQueen raised his eyebrows.

"You."

"Don't forget it. Learn those five, uncircle them, and keep circling into the next chapter. Friday morning, back here. Same time."

The hallway was still mostly empty, and Travis sat on the floor in front of his locker and opened the book. Long lines of words tromped across the pages like columns of ants. McQueen found the swamp in those words, and he took Travis there with him. Not just into the nighttime snowstorm, but into the fox itself, moving through the winter woods and hearing and smelling that mysterious animal world. The lines of ink on the page were a secret code. For the first time, Travis wanted to crack it. More than anything.

"Travicus! What've you got there?"

Travis flipped the book cover-side-down as he scrambled to his feet.

"Why are you here so early?"

"Just had some breakfast," said Velveeta. "Gotta get my recommended daily amount of vitamins and minerals. But you're never here early—weird number one. And you're sitting on the floor, reading—weird number two. It's Bradley's influence, isn't it? He's been sucking you away from the church of the homeworkless?"

"No." Travis put the book in his locker. "I just got here early."

"Because you love school so much, right? Me too. Can't wait for another day of learning. Let's go get smart."

They walked together to Ms. Gordon's room. Velveeta's scarf of the day was golden and brown with some dark greens, faded like they were underwater. Every day he looked forward to seeing her scarf. So far she hadn't repeated one time.

Velveeta was still in McQueen's office having her individual conference when the lunch bell rang, so Travis got to the table first.

"Hey," said Bradley, sitting across from him. "Mind if I sit here?"

Travis shrugged and took a bite of pizza.

"So." Bradley ripped the Velcro on his lunch box. "Chad Cormick said Velveeta's your woman. He said you'll beat the crap out of anybody who looks at her."

Travis stared at Bradley. That sounded a lot better than "crazy bluefish," even if it wasn't true.

"So she is, right? Your girlfriend?"

"I told you before. We're just friends."

"Hi, boys." Velveeta's voice popped behind Travis. "Were you talking about me?"

Travis choked on a bite of pizza as Velveeta set her tray down next to his.

Bradley knocked on the table and said in a deep voice, "Hey, open up." Then he answered himself in a nasal voice. "What's the password?"

He switched back to the deep voice—"Password? Oh, man, I forgot"—and continued to rattle lines about a password back and forth in the two voices.

"Bradley!" yelled Velveeta, waving her hands in front of his face. "Are you okay? Are you having a seizure?"

"No," said Bradley in his normal voice. "It's from a game, the old *Halo*. It's funny."

"You're a freak show," said Velveeta. "But entertaining."

"Do you play?" Bradley asked.

"No," said Velveeta. "Is that what you do for fun?"

"I can't right now. I'm cut off."

"Why?"

"Because it drives my dad crazy. He said if I talked

about a game that wasn't football, Monopoly, or charades one more time, he'd yank them all. I forgot, and did, and he did."

"Wow, that must have been very traumatic for you. Why aren't you sitting with your buddies over there? I'm sure they'd be much more sympathetic to your sad story."

Bradley and Velveeta punched words back and forth across the table so fast, they didn't even land. Like a tennis ball that never hit the court.

"Those guys are no fun since I can't play," said Bradley. "I went over to Reed's last night, and he and Jake were all about how they'd pwn me if I was playing, but they're only saying that because I can't."

"Whatever that means," said Velveeta. "If you were at Reed's house, why couldn't you play? Would Reed's parents rat you out?"

"I wouldn't lie to my parents."

"Really? Never? What about you, Travis?" The sound of his name jerked Travis out of the bleachers and into the game. "Do you lie?"

"About what?" he asked.

"Anything," said Velveeta. "Do you lie to your parents?"

"I don't say anything to them."

"Predictable," said Velveeta. "Bradley is Mr. Honesty America. Travis the stealth boy keeps his mouth shut, and Velveeta lies to anyone who will listen. We should start a superhero team."

"Maybe," said Bradley. "But maybe you're lying about lying."

"Maybe I'm not," said Velveeta. "Anyway, you don't have to worry about me and Travis here tempting you with any illegal electronics. We don't even know what you're talking about half the time, right, Travissimo?"

"I don't," said Travis. Even if he wanted those games, he'd never have them, and even if he had them, he'd rather be on Velveeta's team than Bradley's in any game.

"Okay, then tell me what you guys talk about so I can talk about it with my dad and prove I can talk about something besides games, and then he'll let me back online."

"Oh, so that's why you're sitting with the white-trash club?" said Velveeta. "Trying to learn our language so you can normal up to Daddy?"

"No, I—"

"Sorry we couldn't give you more to work with, Bradley. Try us again tomorrow—we'll talk about shoplifting. Your daddy will love that."

She walked away, and Bradley turned to Travis in half a panic.

"I didn't mean it like that," he said. "I like you guys."

"You like Velveeta."

"I do. Can you tell her I didn't mean it like that?"

"Tell her yourself," said Travis.

Velveeta on WEDNESDAY

I went home after working at the library and the madre wanted to play cribbage, but I hate playing with her when she's that drunk. She started in with, "What am I going to do when you leave me?"

The thing is, what IS she going to do when I leave? I mean, I'm leaving someday, right? I don't have to live in this trailer court forever, do I? And what happens when she gets sick — not hung over, but really sick? Buttface Jimmy only comes over when he needs something, not when she needs something.

Then I look at Bradley, with his nice new clothes and shiny white Nikes and green and gold braces on his teeth. He is so well taken care of — who cares if he's the biggest dork in America? I bet his parents already have him enrolled in some fancy college. I bet they check his homework every night. I bet they tuck him into bed. I bet his mommy sings him lullabies.

I've been reading this book of McQueen's. It's about a girl named Liesel whose mother dumped her with strangers. She's super-smart, but she can't read. Not even a little. The way she learns how is by circling words in a book.

I was in the middle of that part today and I looked over at Travis, and he was concentrating like crazy on that book with the fox on the cover. Writing in it with a pencil. He didn't look up one time the whole period.

Plus he was at school early, sitting on the floor with that book and a pencil, and he tried to hide it when I walked up.

Plus he has passed every single time we read in Gordon's class. Every time. I've never heard him read anything.

Plus he was so hostile about doing that social-studies project together, but as soon as that was over, he got normal again.

And biggest plus: that day in front of the library. He asked what it was, even though the sign was right there, and I gave him a "Can't you read?" snotty answer. That's when he acted like I'd thrown a rock at him.

I think Travis is circling words.

Chapter Fourteen

Travis kept thinking about what Velveeta said about lying all the time. Did she really lie all the time? If she did, how was he supposed to know what to believe? Maybe he was stupid for believing any of it.

The next day at lunch, she pushed the thick book she'd been reading into the middle of the table. "Do you know what this book is about?" The picture on the cover was a dark curvy line of dominoes, with a finger ready to push the first one over.

"You said it's about death."

"Yeah, but it's about something else, too. There's this girl in it, and she can't read. She's super-smart, but she never learned, and then in the book she learns how."

A hot fire lit up under Travis's face.

"It's so great," said Velveeta, "the way she learns. Not with baby books, but with a book about digging graves."

"You want my cookie?" he asked.

If only Bradley would show up. Where was he, anyway?

"You know that fox book you carry around?" she asked. "Are you circling words in there? I just wondered because the girl in here kind of reminds me of you, and that's what she's doing, so I wondered if that's what you're doing. Besides, McQueen is the one who made me start reading this book."

"He told you." Travis narrowed his eyes at McQueen, over at the teachers' table.

"No!" yelped Velveeta. "He didn't say anything. He's a buttinski, not a blabbermouth. I figured it out myself, and I swear, I won't tell anyone. I think it's super-cool, just like Liesel in the book. And she's got this friend named Rudy, and they steal stuff together. Maybe we can go steal some stuff, too. What do you want to steal?"

Travis was sweating so hard, it ran down his sides. He bit his lip so his teeth wouldn't chatter.

"Travis, really, it's okay," Velveeta said. "If it's none of my business, and if you want me to shut up, just knock on the table three times. If you don't want me to shut up but you still want me to eat your cookie, knock twice. If you want to give me an extra twenty dollars today if I kiss you in front of everyone, knock once. If you — "

Travis held up his hand.

"That's not a knock," said Velveeta.

Travis shook his head.

"I understand the sign language of the Travatoni tribe. I will stop talking."

"I gotta go." He picked up his tray.

"The bell didn't ring yet," she called after him.

He hid out in the library for the rest of the lunch period, taking deep breaths to keep from freaking out. She knew. There was no way to make her not know, because now she knew. She said she wouldn't tell anyone, but what if that was a lie?

All afternoon, he kept the fox with him. He circled words into the second chapter and went over his list of five words again and again, writing them on his palm with his finger. Tracing them in deep.

Velveeta came by his locker after school.

"Can I see the book?"

"No," said Travis.

"Please?"

Travis put the book in his backpack, pulled on his jacket, and slammed his locker.

"Don't be mad." Velveeta followed him. "I won't tell anyone, I swear. And I really do think it's cool."

"Yeah, but you lie all the time, remember?"

Velveeta stopped. When Travis got to the door, he

turned and leaned on it as he pushed his way out. She was still standing where he'd left her, in the middle of the hall, kids streaming around her like she was an island.

Their eyes met, and she turned away. Limping, almost.

Travis pushed out the door. The air was dense and sullen, the sky a gray muddle, like Travis's stomach. He'd hurt her. Not a bloody nose or a concussion, but something just as bad.

He turned down the alley and peeked in the park. Nobody there. Travis dropped his backpack and took McQueen's scrap of paper out of his pocket. He leaned against the center pole of the merry-go-round. *Summer, branches, young, night, hunt.* He traced them onto his palm.

"Hey, Travis."

He shoved the paper in his pocket.

"What are you doing?" Bradley tossed down his book bag and sat on the merry-go-round.

"Nothing."

"I want to ask your advice about Velveeta. She got me all wrong at lunch yesterday. How do I tell her that?"

Again, Travis saw Velveeta standing alone in the hall. Even her scarf was drooping.

"I don't know. Just tell her."

"Because the thing is, I do like her. I like her a lot. You know I'm not just sitting by you because my games got yanked, right? Because I'm not. And I don't just like Velveeta. I like you, too. You're cool, but you're not mean."

"I'm not cool," Travis said.

"Yes, you are. Even Chad Cormick thinks you're cool."

"He does?"

"Yup. He said so. He said, 'That Roberts kid is one coolio moolio.' And Reed said maybe you're the Master Chief on a time-regression mission."

"The master who?"

"The Master Chief. He kicked butt way before he got Cortana and MJOLNIR armor. Hey, you know that picnic table by the bridge? Are there some guys there every afternoon?"

"Sometimes," said Travis. "Why?"

"No reason." Bradley kicked the dirt so the merry-go-round started to roll. "So you think I should just tell Velveeta she got it wrong? Or should I not sit by you anymore?"

"I think you should do what you want." Travis grabbed his backpack as he stood. "I gotta go."

"See you tomorrow," said Bradley.

Travis walked slowly through town. So Velveeta got Bradley all wrong. And he got Velveeta wrong. The picnic-table guys hooted and whistled when he walked across the bridge. Travis glanced over at them. Maybe everybody got everybody wrong.

He walked into the house with no Rosco and opened the refrigerator. Sitting on the top shelf, smack in the center, was a twelve-pack of cans, and they weren't Coke.

"Huh." His stomach landed somewhere close to his knees. "So much for that."

He took the fox book out on the back stoop. A moody wind thrashed through the yard. He had just finished erasing the circles around the five words on the first two pages when Grandpa slammed the front door.

"You home?"

"Out here," said Travis.

"How's things?" Grandpa stepped onto the porch. He cracked open a can and tried to light up. The wind blew out the flame, and he had to set the can down and use both hands, making a wind shield. "Learn anything new today?"

"So much for your thirty days, huh?" Travis pointed at the can.

"O'Doul's — nonalcoholic beer," said Grandpa. "See, it says right here."

He put his finger under the tiny-print words.

"Anyway, since when do you care?" He took a deep drag of his cigarette. "It's not easy, you know," he said, the smoke streaming out with his words. "This sobriety thing. I could use a little support."

"What's so hard about it? Just don't drink the stuff."

Grandpa slammed the can on the concrete step, and liquid fizzed up and over. Alcoholic or not, it sure smelled like beer.

"That easy, huh? Is that what you think?"

Grandpa poked him in the shoulder, and Travis moved away. Grandpa reached over and poked again. Like he used to do when Travis was little and didn't want to go to school.

"Don't you crawl off in a corner and cry!" he used to yell. "If you're mad, get out here and make some fists."

And he'd keep poking until Travis slapped his hand away. Then he'd laugh and poke again. The poking went on until Travis made real fists and swung hard. Then Grandpa would put up his palms and get Travis to slug them over and over, hard enough to make solid smacks. After that, he'd sling an arm around Travis's neck, and the three of them — Travis, Grandpa, and Rosco — would go out to the swamp. That was a long, long time ago.

"You think you got it so bad," said Grandpa. "Boo-hoo, poor Travis."

He poked again. Travis clenched his teeth hard. He picked up the book and stepped around Grandpa.

"I've got homework."

He slammed the screen door on his way through, went into his tiny box of a bedroom, and shut the door. He circled words in chapter two until Grandpa went to bed. Then he made himself a piece of cheese toast for dinner.

Velveeta on THURSDAY

I can't believe Travis thought I was lying about thinking it's cool that he's learning to read. I wouldn't lie about something like that. Not ever. So that's his secret, not dying of leukemia. I want us to be friends like Liesel and Rudy in *The Book Thief,* only now I'm not sure if we get to be any kind of friends at all. He didn't want his secret busted. I should have kept my mouth shut. I still can't believe he thought I was lying, though. Ouch.

Later—
The madre came banging on the door while I was writing and just about scared me out of my skin. I didn't let her in, but I went back over to our place with her because she was crying. She said I'd rather spend my time in an empty trailer where an old man died than be with my own flesh and blood, and why am I so mean to her? I hate it when she's like that. It makes me feel so bad. She asked me to stay home from school tomorrow and hang out with her.

How did I ever get to school in the first place? Somebody must have made me go to kindergarten the first time, right? Or did I just wake up one morning and say, "Hey, Ma, I'm five. Guess it's time for me to go to school."?

I don't remember that.

I remember the first time I came to your trailer, though. You gave me a cookie. How old was I? I think I was in first grade. I couldn't read yet, because I remember you reading to me.

I also remember when you bought me a toothbrush. And I remember you drilling me on the multiplication tables and spelling words. Good thing you weren't some old perv or something, because it's not like anyone was making sure you weren't. The madre did call you a perv once — I never told you that, but she did. I hit her in the face, and whoa, she yanked my hair and smacked me a good one. Didn't know that, did you?

Calvin. Do you think you could come back and haunt this place, just a little bit? Please?

Chapter Fifteen

Friday morning, Travis closed his eyes as McQueen read from the fox book. The story took him away from school, from Grandpa, from Velveeta's hurt eyes, and from the hard work of learning word by word. He didn't believe he would ever be able to read smoothly like that, but he had learned five words. He knew them now, for sure. Five words wasn't a lot, but it was five more than he knew last week.

When McQueen finished reading, he wrote something down.

"What's this word?" He flipped the paper around so Travis could see.

"Night," said Travis immediately. That had been on his list.

"This one?"

T. ight. A smile started somewhere in Travis's gut and spread over his whole body.

"Tight?"

McQueen grinned. "This one?"

"Lll. Light."

Travis whipped through the new list, six words.

"Why isn't *bite* on here?"

"Brilliant question," said McQueen. "It's not here because the English language is filled with sinkholes and blind traps. Stick with these six for the weekend, and we'll tackle *bite* later. I've got something else for you to think about, too."

"What?" Travis took the book back.

"It's time for you to start dealing with your other classes. Ms. Gordon can set you up to use the Kurzweil in the library while everyone else is reading."

"The what?"

"It's assistive technology. Reads the textbook out loud to you and highlights the words so you can follow along. It'll help you with writing, too."

"A special-ed thing," said Travis.

"Yes, and why are you making that face? I don't know if you qualify or not, but you need extra help. All you have to do is ask, and you'll get it."

Travis's third-grade teacher had tried to get him into

special ed. She made Grandpa come to school for a meeting, and he came home mad. He said Travis had better get it together and pay attention. Nobody said anything about special ed after that, but he had to go to lipsticky Mrs. Keatley three days a week. Everybody knew what that meant.

Travis wasn't going to ask Ms. Gordon for the Kurtz-thing. He might as well put a bluefish sticker on his head. He got up to leave, but McQueen stopped him on his way out the door.

"Nice job with those words, Mr. Roberts. I'm impressed."

McQueen's words glowed warm around Travis as he headed for his locker. If he worked faster and harder, maybe he could catch up and he wouldn't need any special ed. He just wanted to be regular.

Travis got to first period early and watched the door. Velveeta came in and didn't say anything, just quietly sat behind him.

"Hey," he said.

"Hey."

She took out a pen and drew tiny tornado spirals on the back of her notebook. Maybe he should say he was sorry for saying that she lied. But she was the one who said she lied all the time. How was he supposed to know what to believe?

As soon as he faced front, she tapped her pen on the top of his head.

"Just so you know," she whispered, "I don't lie about everything. I was lying when I said that."

As Travis turned to respond, something landed with a light thud on Velveeta's desk, slid across, and dropped to the floor. Travis picked up a papier-mâché spider leg. He threw it to Megan, who was waving from the other side of the room. Another leg flew to the front corner. Jeremy Matthews was busy in the back, detaching all eight legs from his Paleozoic project and launching them into the air. Another one came to Travis and he caught it and threw it to Chad.

"Are you protecting me from the prehistoric spider legs?" asked Velveeta.

"Kind of." Travis stabbed his arm high to catch the one Chad threw over his head.

"Travis Roberts." Ms. Gordon closed the door as she walked into the room. "Stop."

She held out her hand for the leg, and he gave it to her. The other legs had all disappeared under desks. Ms. Gordon dropped the leg into the garbage can and started talking about the next assignment as though nothing had happened.

Velveeta poked Travis in the neck a few times during class, and every poke was a relief. Maybe she really wouldn't tell anyone about the word circling.

"You know I wasn't lying, right?" she said as soon as the bell rang. "About thinking it's cool what you're doing?"

Travis shrugged.

"Because I wasn't. I wouldn't lie about that, not ever. Sit by me at lunch, right?"

He believed her because of how she'd looked in the hallway the day before. And because he wanted to. He spent the rest of the morning going over his new words and looking forward to lunch.

Bradley came up behind Travis in the lunch line.

"I'm going to do like you said and do what I want. Even if she decimates me. I mean, what can she do? So she makes me feel stupid—so what? Maybe she'll get everyone in the lunchroom to make fun of me. That wouldn't kill me, right?"

Travis picked up his lunch, quesadillas and beans and rice and a snickerdoodle, without answering. Just like Velveeta, Bradley could have a whole conversation all by himself.

When they got to the table, Velveeta said, "So, Bradley's slumming today. Eating the school lunch, even."

"You've got it all wrong about me." Bradley set his tray on the table and stood with his arms crossed.

"Oh, really," said Velveeta. The words sounded like a sword sliding out of its sheath. "Tell me, Bradley, what do I have so very wrong?"

"The whole thing about me slumming. That's mean and plus, not true."

"How do I know that?" asked Velveeta.

"Because I said so and I don't lie."

"Never? Never never, you never lie, not once, not ever?"

"No. Look, you don't like me — that's okay — I'll leave, but I didn't want you thinking something wrong about why I wanted to hang out with you."

He picked up his tray and started to walk away.

"Wait, Bradley," Velveeta said. "I don't not like you that much."

Bradley stopped. Velveeta looked at Travis and nodded, as if he'd said something.

"And actually," she said, "I know you weren't lying, okay? Come on. Sit back down."

"So we're clear, then?" Bradley turned to face her. "I didn't mean anything bad, and you know I don't lie, right?"

"Bradley, we're all very crystal-clear. Aren't you clear, Travis?"

"I'm not in this," said Travis as Bradley sat back down.

"Why are you eating a school lunch?" asked Velveeta, who had already finished off most of hers.

"No good leftovers in the house. Besides, I like quesadillas."

"So if you're not slumming for research, then why are you sitting here? You should be over with Reed and Jake, talking about quadratic equations."

"I like you," said Bradley.

"You are officially out of your mind."

"Why? Travis likes you."

"Travis likes me because he's captured by my feminine wiles. He can't take his eyes off me, can you, Travis? I think we should talk about this every day. Why does everyone like Velveeta? You can make a list of reasons. It'll be a fan club."

"Okay." Bradley got up as the bell rang. "I'll be president. Or no, I'll be secretary. I'll make the list."

Travis followed them out of the lunchroom. Bradley could make his own list, and he should sit somewhere else to do it.

Velveeta came up beside Travis as he stepped out the double doors.

"What are you doing now?"

"Going home."

"Come to the library with me."

"Why?" asked Travis.

"Because it's cold outside and warm in the library. Or are you rushing home to paint words on the wall of your basement?"

"We don't have a basement."

"Well, that's what Liesel does in the book."

"On your left!"

Velveeta leaned into Travis, bumping him off the sidewalk as a couple of skaters rattled by.

"If you come to the library with me, maybe I could help you. Like, go over words and stuff."

Travis shook his head.

"Please?"

"Why would you want to?"

He expected a rapid-fire answer about prostitution or being in love with her or the wrath of Velveeta, but nothing came. When she finally spoke, it was so soft he barely heard.

"Because I want to be part of it." She abruptly turned and walked the other way.

She took big long strides, almost running, her purple-and-blue scarf flowing out behind and catching on the breeze. A few yellow leaves drifted down. He expected her to turn and look at him, but she didn't.

Travis shivered. The breeze had gone cold, and the sky stacked layers of steely gray. He followed Velveeta. She glanced back as she crossed the street, spotted him, and grinned.

"Did you bring the book?" she asked when he caught up.

He nodded and fell into step alongside of her.

As they came up to the library, Travis asked, "How'd you get a job here?"

"It's not an official job. I just put away books and run errands and do what Connie says, and she slips me a cash payment. I think she embezzles it out of the overdue fines. Very stealth and illegal, I'm sure."

"Do you like it?"

"It's better than being punched in the head twelve times."

She held the door open for Travis. The place was crowded and squat, with low ceilings, and slam-crammed full of books, like McQueen's office to the fifteenth power. Velveeta grabbed the shoulder of his sweatshirt and led him zigging around some shorter shelves toward the back corner. He almost tripped over a toddler on the floor.

"Velveeta!" A tiny lady with spiked white hair and an eyebrow ring came out of the back office. "What are you doing here? It's not Saturday. Wait, I bet I know. You want a nice book, don't you? Here, I'll get you one."

Velveeta turned to Travis and said, "She's a book pusher. Cops have busted her twelve times, but she always gets out on a plea."

"Who's this?"

"Connie, this is Travis," said Velveeta. "We're going to study. Can we use the study room, or is somebody in there?"

"All yours," said Connie.

Velveeta dragged Travis into a tiny room and shut the door. He pulled the fox book out of his backpack, realizing suddenly that she would see all those circled words. Baby words. Words everyone knew.

"You know, in *The Book Thief,* Liesel barely even knew the alphabet," said Velveeta. "She had to start from the beginning. But she did it. She worked at it super hard. She's amazing. Come on, let me see the book."

She held her hand out across the table and wiggled her fingers, asking for it. Travis met her eyes. Brown and quiet, not snicking or rolling, not laughing. She waggled her fingers again, and he handed the book over.

"These are the words you're working on?" She pulled out the scraps of paper he'd stuck in the book.

Travis nodded. She turned the papers so they faced Travis and said, "Let's hear them."

He read both lists and he didn't miss one word. Velveeta swept the papers off the table.

"Okay, you need a real challenge."

She pulled a notebook out of her backpack and started copying words from the fox book.

"Whoa. I can't learn all those."

"Yes, you can. You're on the Velveeta train now, and we're leaving the station. This word is *unwise* — here, say it."

She jabbed her pen point at the first word on the list.

"Unwise." Travis tried to plant it in his head.

Velveeta held up her fist. Travis looked at it, then at her face, then back at her fist.

"Do something to it! Tap it or bang it or do some hand-jive thingy already so we can get back to work."

Travis sledgehammered her fist so hard it dipped to the table and bounced back up.

"Finally, some teamwork here. Now, this long word, here, this says *desperately*, as in, Travis wanted desperately to declare his true love for Velveeta. Say it."

"Desperately," said Travis. "That's an awfully big word."

"Stop whining. You have to learn ten words before you

can leave. Here, this one says *murky*, as in, Ms. Gordon's class is a murky Mesozoic swamp where papier-mâché spiders rule. Say it — *murky*."

"Murky." Travis cracked a smile. "I bet you can't come up with something for every word."

"Oh, yeah? Watch me!"

Velveeta rattled off strings of crazy sentences for every word on the list. By the end, Travis mostly knew them. Velveeta drilled him back through to make sure.

"Isn't this boring for you?" Travis put the book in his backpack, and picked up McQueen's lists from the floor.

"Boring? Are you kidding? This is fun, a-barrel-of-funky-monkeys fun. I'd love to see you wow McQueen on Monday. Can I come and watch?"

"No."

"Okay, fine, I'll just plant a camera and a mic." Velveeta stepped into the main library room. "You make me miss all the good stuff. By Monday, you'll be stealing books."

"Who's stealing my books?" asked Connie, coming up behind them.

"I didn't," said Travis.

"Get a library card, and you won't have to steal," called Connie as they pushed out the door.

Travis kept Velveeta's piece of paper out as he walked home, going over and over the words so he wouldn't forget. All together, that made twenty-one words. All his.

Velveeta on a Fine FRIDAY

It's so amazing and fantabulous. Travis learned all those words today, and I helped him. That made me want to explode and happy-dance with how good it felt, pouring those words into his brain and watching them stick. He's not dumb as a post — he's super-smart. Smarter than Liesel the book thief, maybe. He's going to be whipping through that fox book in no time.

Plus, here's something funny that happened in school. In reading, I was watching Travis working on his book, and then I looked over at McQueen, and he looked back, zippo-zappo, right in the eyeballs, and I looked down at *The Book Thief* on my desk and up at him, and he almost smiled, but not quite. Just enough to let me know that he knew that I knew that he knew that ... He's smooth, that McQueen.

Chapter Sixteen

Travis headed out Saturday around noon. He had *Haunt Fox* in his backpack and baloney in his pocket. Out of the house before Grandpa got home from work.

The day before, walking home on a cloud of word happiness, he'd actually hoped Grandpa would ask if he'd learned anything at school that day. He wanted to say YES and mean it. But Grandpa walked in the door, tossed Travis a doughnut, and spent the evening sucking down O'Doul's and watching TV. Didn't ask anything. He didn't go to his AA meeting. Hadn't gone all week, in fact, or said one word to Travis since poking him Thursday night. Looked like he was back to not liking chatterboxes.

The day was gray and sullen, the sun hidden. Moisture hung thick on the air, and Travis found it hard to get a full deep breath. When he got close to the dog's house, he high-low whistled. The dog came roaring down the driveway.

"Hang on, hang on." Travis pulled the plastic bag out of his pocket. The dog quit barking as soon as Travis opened the bag. He could smell that baloney and didn't want to scare it away.

Travis tossed him a piece, and he caught it on the float — *chomp sloop* — and it was gone. Travis tossed him the other one. *Slurp*, gone. His long pink tongue swooshed across his teeth, splashing slobber. Travis turned the empty bag inside out and held it at arm's length. The dog dainty-stepped closer and carefully nosed it, licked it, and waved the tip of his tail. He was a nice-looking dog when he wasn't all hair-up lip-snarled. Black with a white chest like a clean shirtfront. Pointed stand-up ears and a sharp nose, and a long narrow tail with a white tip on the end.

"When you're not doing that snarly thing, you look pretty good," said Travis. "But you've still got some drool dripping there."

The dog cocked his head and geared his tail up to a full wag.

"You wouldn't want to go for a walk with me, would you?"

Travis turned to walk away, patting his thigh as he went.

"C'mon, boy. C'mon."

He trotted a little, clapping his hands.

"C'mon."

The dog watched Travis like he was a cartoon on TV. Travis squatted, whistled, and held out his hands.

"Just for a little bit? Just up to the next corner? C'mere, boy."

Travis patted the ground in front of him. The dog looked at the spot with all attention, as if he wanted to understand what the problem was.

"No go, huh? You've got your home and your people — you don't need a walk with me."

A huge rock hulked at the bottom of the driveway, on the other side of the ditch. Taller than Travis, wider than his spread arms.

"What if I just sat there behind your rock for a while and looked over my words? Would you mind?"

The dog stood in place, allowing Travis to approach. He found a flat spot where he could use the rock for a backrest and be completely hidden from the road. The dog didn't growl or bark, but he watched Travis's every move.

"Want to come over here?" asked Travis. "Sit by me? I'll read words to you."

It came out so easy, talking to the dog. Rosco never minded chatterboxing. He'd gaze up at Travis and tick his skinny tail back and forth, waiting for more.

Travis took out his lists and said the words out loud.

He mixed up the order and practiced again. Up and down the lists. The dog edged closer and lay down, nose on his paws, about ten feet away. Listening.

"Not gonna rip my face off if I get one wrong, are you? Oh, wait, you started to wag again — I saw it."

Travis started from the top again. Suddenly, the dog jumped to his feet, ears pricked and tail wagging.

"Larry!" The voice was creaky, like it didn't get used much. "Larry, where are you?"

The dog dashed up the drive. Travis sat perfectly still. If the person came down the drive and looked right, he'd be caught. He was partially hidden by high grass, but not completely. He closed the book and scooted back, trying to ease out of sight, but before he could get all the way around the rock, Larry appeared. Travis froze.

An old woman with a cane walked behind Larry. She moved slowly, her eyes on the ground.

"Where were you?" she asked. "Chasing a squirrel? Barking at the mail?"

She moved beyond Travis's view, on the other side of the rock. The mailbox opened and closed.

"Nothing but bills. Come on, let's get in before it starts raining."

She came back into view and looked up, searching the sky from one horizon to the other. Travis held his breath. She'd see him any minute, and what would he say? "I wanted to sit by your rock"? "I like your dog"?

She pulled herself up the slope on her cane, Larry at

her side. A raindrop fell on Travis's hand, and another on his cheek. A few more spattered on the book. As soon as the woman and Larry were out of sight, he put the book in his backpack and crawled to the other side of the rock. No cars were coming from either direction, so he walked out to the road.

The rain came down in fat, warm drops. He went the long way around into town and stopped at the library, hoping Velveeta might still be there. By the time he got to the door, the rain had turned cold.

"Did you come to get a library card?" Connie asked when he stuck his dripping head in the door.

"No, just looking for Velveeta."

"She left already. Do you want to come in and dry off? Maybe find a nice book or two?"

"No, thanks." He backed out and put his jacket over his backpack so *Haunt Fox* wouldn't get wet.

Cold trickles ran down the back of his neck. As he passed the convenience store, Bradley came out the door carrying a gallon of milk.

"Hey, Travis, why are you walking around in the rain? I got sent out for milk because my parents don't care if I catch pneumonia."

"No reason."

They walked through town together.

"I thought that went pretty well at lunch Friday," said Bradley. "That was funny, the Velveeta Fan Club. You're still not going out with her, right? Still just friends?"

"Why do you care so much?"

"Because I was thinking about asking her to the dance, but I wouldn't if you were going to. I mean, you got there first."

Travis didn't know anything about any dance.

"I've been thinking about it since the posters went up last week and it can't hurt to ask, right? I know she'll say no, but so what? I figure even asking will be interesting, because who knows what she'll say? I'm getting better at sword fighting with her, don't you think?"

They got to Water Street and Bradley stopped.

"So you don't mind, right? If I ask her?"

Travis stood there with his hands jammed in his pockets, shivering. Bradley had on a nice rain jacket with the hood pulled up, and hiking boots. Travis's socks were soggy.

"I didn't think you would, but I just wanted to make sure, because you and I are getting to be friends, too, right?"

Just then, Travis didn't feel very friendly. He wished Bradley would go away and stay there.

"Okay, then, see you later, Trav."

Bradley turned down Water. Travis's feet squished in his shoes as he walked up the hill toward home.

Velveeta on a Soggy, Sucky SUNDAY

Yesterday when I got home from work, the butt's truck was in the drive. I would have gone straight to your trailer, only it was pouring rain and I was soaked all the way to my underwear, and — stupid me — I haven't been keeping clothes at your trailer, but from now on I'm going to, for sure.

So I opened the door and there he was, drunko skunko, sitting on the floor with his head in the lap of the madre, bawling. The madre looked up at me like I was, I don't know, a stranger. Like I was interrupting. Mean-faced, like she hated me.

So, wet or not, I came over here and double-bolted. And stayed here overnight, wrapped up in a towel and a blanket. Nobody even bothered to see if I'm okay. I could have been out in the rain, catching my death of icy-rain cold.

The madre is so many different people. Am I going to get the face-slapping mean madre or the fun card-playing madre or the crying-in-her-beer madre? I never know. Sometimes it makes my head want to spin off. And why doesn't she just kick Jimmy's lazy no-good butt away from here for good?

I wonder what Travis is doing today. I wonder what it's like at his house. I wonder if he learned any new words. Maybe he has really nice parents and I could move in there. They could hide me in the basement and feed me on leftover bread crusts. Only they don't have a basement.

Chapter Seventeen

Travis had all twenty-one words ready to rip for McQueen on Monday. He ran through the whole list, and McQueen just about did a dance in his chair.

"You've earned yourself a mid-quarter A in reading," he said. "And wait till you see the new list I've got for you. You're going to love this one!"

It was all trees. Maple, birch, aspen, oak, hemlock, pine.

"Do you know these trees?" asked McQueen. "Can you pick them out in the woods?"

No problem. Travis could close his eyes and picture each one — trunks, leaves, fall colors, spring buds and candles.

"Would you be able to draw any of them?" asked McQueen. "Nothing fancy, just a sketch?"

Travis nodded.

"Great. By Wednesday, draw me a sketch of each one. Put a sign up in front with the name of the tree. All those words are on page one."

When Travis got to first period, of course Velveeta wanted to see his new list of words. He told her what McQueen wanted.

"And you can do that? You actually know what those trees are?"

"Sure."

"I knew it all along," she muttered. "Hiding behind that 'I can't read' business, and there you are with your oversize brain. You're not an undercover cop — you're an undercover forest ranger."

All through first period, she passed him stick drawings with the word printed beneath. A tiger, an octopus, a giraffe, and something he finally figured out was a camel. He kept the scraps in a neat stack and put them in his pocket when the bell rang.

Between classes, Travis stopped and looked at the dance posters. He didn't want to go to any dance, but maybe Velveeta did. What if he, Travis, was the one who shouldn't sit with them at lunch? Bradley fired plenty of words at her, more than Travis could come up with in a month.

When he got through the lunch line, he was surprised to see Bradley sitting with Reed and Jake. Velveeta waited for him, with the book from McQueen out on the table.

"I banished Bradley today so we could lunch in peace." She tapped the cover of the book. "The reason this book is called *The Book Thief* is because the girl who can't read keeps stealing books."

"Why?"

"She can't help herself. And then all kinds of things happen to her because of stealing them. And because she can read now."

"Just like that, she can read now?"

"No, not just like that. She had to work at it for a long time."

"Oh."

"But she did, and then she ends up reading out loud to everyone in the bomb shelter. She saves the day by being able to read. I wonder what day you're going to save, Traverelli. Maybe you'll save us from terrorists."

"I doubt it."

"Then maybe you'll give me your Rice Krispies bar and save me from malnutrition."

"Maybe not." He grinned at her.

"I love it when you're mysterious. I guess this time

maybe means *no*, since you're already—oh, it's in the mouth. That's a definite no."

They picked up their trays and headed to the garbage can, Travis still swallowing the last of the Rice Krispies bar. Velveeta's orange-and-yellow scarf splashed color over her shoulder, brightness laid across the smooth dark of her hair. A ray of sun through the window lit her head, so he could see the color of each hair separately—some brown, some dark red. He wanted to touch, to see if her hair would be as silky soft as he imagined.

She turned around and bumped him, almost knocking the tray loose from his hands.

"You're crowding me, Travicus."

He fumbled and dropped his tray as she stepped around him. His plate clattered on the floor, and the fork flew behind the garbage can, and everyone nearby applauded.

"Clumsy much?" Cassidy pushed past him to dump her tray.

Travis's face was so hot, he was glad to have a reason to kneel on the floor. He slowly picked up his plate and silverware. By the time he got everything sorted and thrown away, Velveeta was gone.

He drifted through the afternoon on that splash of color. The way the sun came in at just the angle to catch the red in her hair. Usually things indoors didn't look that good.

He was just opening his locker after the last bell when Velveeta came skidding up.

"Listen to this," she said. "You'll never guess who just asked me out."

Travis's stomach dropped.

"Bradley Whistler." Velveeta nodded. "To the dance. Can you believe that?"

"What'd you say?" asked Travis.

"What should I have said?"

"I don't know. Whatever you want, I guess."

Travis turned back to his locker. He took as much time as he could, straightening his books and pens, and then pulled his hoodie out and put it on. Velveeta stood there with her hands on her hips, watching him. She fired a direct gaze into his eyes, like a super-power telescope. He looked down so she wouldn't see his face getting red.

"I told him I'd think about it," she said. "Are you coming to the library with me?"

"What for?"

"Words! Come on, we'll go over the ones I passed you this morning."

A new wave of September heat radiated up from the sidewalk. Travis didn't really feel like doing words, but he wanted her to make him laugh, and call him Travasaurus. He wanted her to say she'd never go to a dance with Bradley in a million years. He kicked a rock in front of them, hoping she'd kick it next. She didn't.

Once they got to the library, Velveeta was all business. "Let's see the book."

Travis handed it over.

"Look, the whole first paragraph is uncircled! You're ready to read it."

He shook his head. Going down a list, one word at a time, that was one thing. But to read a sentence out loud, thrashing through wave after wave of those words? He was not ready for that.

"Shut up!" said Velveeta. "You know every word here. Come on, read it!"

Travis shook his head harder.

"Okay, wait. I know. We'll do it a line at a time. I'll read it, then you read it back. You can do that."

The last part sounded like Mrs. Keatley. *Come on, Travis. You can do THAT.*

Velveeta read the first line, bubbling the words out like liquid candy, easy easy. She handed the book to him. He looked at that first line and didn't see any words. Just a stream of black marks. He closed the book.

"Travis, come on. You didn't even try."

Try. That word torched fire-hot. He took the book and shoved it into his backpack.

"I've got to go."

"I can't believe you're not even going to try."

Travis stepped back, away from her, away from the table, away from everything he wanted to hit or throw. He snatched his backpack and walked out. Her words and the way she said them burned through his chest.

Try. Stupid bluefish, that's all he'd ever be. Thought a few words meant he could read. *TRY, Travis. Can't you at least try?* He never should have told her about the lists of words. It would just give her and Bradley something to laugh about when they went to the dance.

Velveeta on MONDAY

I was mad before we even got to the library because when I told Travis about Bradley asking me to the dance, he acted like he couldn't care less. Not like I thought he'd say, "No, go with me instead," because that would be un-Travis-like. But I did think he'd say something, or at least make a face.

Because of how it was at lunch when I almost smacked him chinside with my tray. I thought he was reaching out to touch my hair. Like in a romantic-movie way. I get it now why people say someone is hot because all of a sudden Travis made me have a fever. Kawoof, furnace on.

Look, bottom line, I gotta get real here. Travis would never like me in a romantic-movie way. Not Vida Wojciehowski, Russet Lowlife Trailer-Trash Loser and half sister of Jimmy the butt. You know what Travis was doing when I thought he was reaching for my hair? He was flicking away a trailer-court cootie.

Still *Velveeta*, on TUESDAY MORNING

Jimmy came over for dinner, so I spent the night here at your place. I hate my life. I especially hate how I feel when Jimmy's around, like the scummiest of scum-sludge bottom-feeder bad.

It stormed all night. I tried to remember what you used to say about how storms are magical and beautiful and awesome. But the thunder growled and barked, and I was all by myself and the electricity went off, so I couldn't watch a movie, and I couldn't find a candle or a flashlight. I started to feel like a bad thing was out there, bamming on the sides of your trailer. Howling at me. Every time I looked at a window, I expected Jack Nicholson's face to show up saying "Heeeeeeere's Johnny," and then he'd chase me through mountains of snow with an ax. I shoved some furniture in front of the door in case the double bolt broke.

Now it's light outside, sort of. At least it's not night anymore, but it's still stormy. The lights are back on, but I don't know what time it is. You know what? I'm not leaving here until Jimmy's truck is gone. I think I will have a Velveeta movie day.

Chapter Eighteen

Travis let the gray drizzle fall on him. He didn't want to go to school, and he couldn't stay home. Grandpa was still in bed and was probably going to miss work. Good thing Travis hadn't gotten all on board with Grandpa's changes, because everything looked to be going off board pretty fast. Grandpa hadn't made dinner in days, they were running out of groceries, and all the asking about homework had stopped. The whole thing had lasted, what, maybe a month?

Travis shoved himself away from the bridge railing with a sigh. He dragged his feet through town. For a while there, he'd even thought he could be a new Travis. But really, everything was the same, especially him. Same old bluefish.

He got to school late, after the first bell. On his way to social studies, he ran into McQueen.

"Mr. Roberts, pick your head up there and look around—oh. Something wrong?"

Travis shrugged.

"Problem with the reading?"

McQueen could make mud clump up in Travis's throat like nobody else.

"Come by after fourth period. Bring the book, and we'll see what tripped you up." McQueen nodded, making his eyes big. "Really, we'll fix it."

Travis paused outside Gordon's room. If Velveeta poked him in the neck, he'd just tell her to quit it. She could mind her own business for once. Her seat was empty, though, and relief washed all over him along with a taste of disappointment.

Bradley snagged Travis in the hall between bells.

"Where's Velveeta?" he asked. "Is she sick?"

"I don't know."

At least Bradley didn't know, either.

"I'll sit by you at lunch, okay?"

"Can't, I'm busy," said Travis.

Good thing he had McQueen. Anything was better than listening to Bradley talk about Velveeta. After fourth period, McQueen sat on the desk in front of him, feet on the chair.

"So what's the problem, Mr. Roberts? Something must have happened. Give me a clue. Sounds like?"

"It's not reading," said Travis. "I mean sure, I learned some words. But when I look at the page, they don't look like anything."

"Ah," said McQueen. "You tried to jump ahead."

Wasn't Travis's idea to jump ahead. That was Velveeta's idea.

"Hm. If you insist on jumping, let's make a jump you can do. Because getting discouraged is not on the program. Wait right here."

McQueen came back from his office with a bright-orange-and-green book. He opened it in the middle and pointed at the sentence above the picture.

"Read this."

"The. Bl. Blue. Dog. Is. In." said Travis.

"Good. Now do it again."

McQueen made him do it three times. Then he said, "Read it like you're telling me something I need to know."

"The blue dog is in."

"Read it like your hair's on fire."

"The blue dog is in." Travis said it a bit louder, a bit faster.

McQueen grinned and closed the book. "Okay, that probably *is* how you'd say it if your hair was on fire. Anyway, that's what most kids learn to read on. Took you maybe three minutes."

"But that's a book for little kids."

"Right. Remember when you asked why we're not using an easier book? Because you're not a child, and this is too easy. We're using a book at your level, and it's hard, and you're doing just fine. Now, go get some lunch."

Travis was halfway out the door when McQueen stopped him.

"Mr. Roberts, is there anything else bothering you?"

Travis met McQueen's hypno eyes, and a shiver ran over him. He couldn't answer.

"If there's anything I can do, let me know. Meanwhile, show up tomorrow and we'll tackle more of *Haunt Fox*."

As Travis walked home after school, he remembered asking Grandpa for help with homework, way back before he was officially a bluefish. *You're too little for homework. What's wrong with those teachers? Go out and play.* He never asked if Travis's homework was done, not once. Not until he started his whole "I'm in AA. Let's talk about everything" thing. Which was now over.

The front door was unlocked, and Grandpa was in the recliner, watching TV. Travis went directly to the refrigerator. Nothing in there but O'Doul's and ketchup.

"We're out of groceries," he said.

No answer.

"Even milk."

Thick stale smoke filled the house, and several empties cluttered the coffee table.

"Why aren't you at work?"

- 139 -

"'Why aren't you at work?'" Grandpa whined, mocking him. "Is that all you care about, if I'm buying groceries or not? I suppose you expect me to make your dinner. You don't care if I'm sober. You just care who's feeding your mug."

"At least do that," muttered Travis.

"You got something to say, speak up."

"Why bother?" Travis raised his voice. "You don't care."

"I don't care?" Grandpa banged down the footrest of the recliner. "I've been taking care of your butt with no help for the last ten years, and I don't care?"

"You only did it because you had to."

"Oh, yeah? Says who?"

"You. I heard you say it to Dave last summer. You were sitting on the porch. You said you got saddled with me and never had a say in it. It's not my fault you're stuck with me."

"No, but it's your fault you're a shit about it." Grandpa stalked around the counter. "And it's my fault to think it'd make any difference to you if I quit drinking. Here, you're a baby? You need somebody to feed you?"

Grandpa yanked open the cupboard, then the fridge. He squeezed a line of ketchup on a cracker and poked it under Travis's nose.

"There, feed your face on that."

Travis smacked the cracker backhand, and it flew. Then he swung hard, connecting with Grandpa's jaw. Grandpa went down like a bag of rocks. Travis turned away, slapping his hands flat on the counter so they couldn't do anything else.

His face flamed. His breath came ragged and hard. He stared at the faded yellow design beneath his hands.

"Feel any better?" Grandpa's voice came from the floor.

"No." Travis said it to the counter.

The fire juice raged through his body. His knees shook so hard he'd fall if he didn't have the counter to hold. He didn't want to see blood or a bruise or a scared-eyed face. The sludge oozed in, cooling the fire and churning his stomach.

"Me neither." Grandpa got to his feet.

Travis kept his eyes down and his hands flat as the keys jingled and the door slammed. The truck started up, and Travis was alone.

Velveeta — Later on TUESDAY in Nightmare Land

I watched *To Kill a Mockingbird* this afternoon. It made me so sad and so lonely because I used to have someone like Atticus and now I don't. I don't have anybody. I fell asleep crying, and somewhere in my sleep, I heard this banging, and I managed to unstick my eyelids, only I thought maybe I was still asleep, because just like in a really bad nightmare, someone was standing in the doorway.

"Who the hell are you, and what are you doing in my father's trailer?"

Sylvia didn't yell it. She said it in this mean, low voice like she was about to slit my throat wide open. She looked even meaner than she did at the funeral. I scrabbled up off the couch and tried to make some words, but I couldn't do it.

"How did you get in here?"

Because I'm stupid and I was barely awake, I pointed at the key on the counter. She grabbed the key and pointed at the door with it.

"Get out of here."

So I did.

Chapter Nineteen

Travis wrenched his eyelids open. Gray light oozed in through the yellow towel, and a growl of thunder slunk around the house. Storming again. Grandpa hadn't come home, still hadn't been there at midnight when Travis went to bed. He untangled himself from the blankets and listened. No sounds. What if Grandpa's jaw was broken, or he'd gotten drunk and arrested or in a crash? What if he never came back?

Then Travis smelled smoke. He rolled out of bed, pulled on sweats, and opened his door. Grandpa sat at the kitchen table. No black eye, no broken jaw. Not even a bruise.

"I heard you whimpering in there," he said. "Bad dream?"

Travis turned into the bathroom. He stayed in the shower for a long time. When he opened the door, Grandpa was still sitting there, staring at him.

"Sit down here, boy," he said. "I've got some things to say."

"I have to get ready for school."

"You've got time. Sit down."

Lightning flashed in the morning gray. A wind breezed through the open window, slicing through the clouds of cigarette smoke. Travis sat across from Grandpa in jeans and no shirt, the wet towel still around his neck. Grandpa flicked his lighter off and on. He stubbed out the last of his butt.

"Whoever taught you to fight did a hell of a job," he said, touching his jaw. "Gave me a goose egg." Looking closer, Travis could see the swelling.

"Sorry."

"No, you're not. Listen, we need to get some things straight here."

Grandpa lit up another cigarette. Travis leaned back and folded his arms across his chest. He didn't want to hear it. Not with dried ketchup still stuck on the wall and a storm outside getting ready to pounce. Thunder snarled past the window.

"We had to move. I was three months behind in rent. Your dad's life insurance is almost gone. This house is cheap, I got the job at the bakery, and AA meetings are close. That's where I went last night."

Relief and irritation swirled through Travis, twisted his stomach. Rent, insurance, AA, whatever. Drinking or not drinking. Rosco was gone. He and Grandpa didn't like each other. That's just how it was.

Grandpa shoved his chair back and walked over to stand at the window, staring out and smoking. The morning sky darkened, as if someone had just thrown a blanket over the barely risen sun.

"That's not really what I have to tell you."

He took a deep drag on his cigarette and then crushed the end as he sat back down. He picked up the lighter and flicked. The flame came up, blue on the inside with bright yellow quivering and dancing at the tip. Something sat heavy on the table between them, something bad. The smell of it filled the room, choking Travis, making it hard to breathe.

"Gotta do it," said Grandpa softly. He set the lighter down, put both hands flat on the table, and looked Travis full in the eyes. "Rosco. I killed him."

The words hit Travis like a slap on the face. He sucked his breath in and held it.

"Didn't mean to. I backed out the drive. I thought he'd gone with you to the swamp."

Travis stared, his air slow-leaking out.

"I didn't even look, and you know how Rosco wouldn't move unless you made him."

Travis shook his head no, but he could see Rosco sprawled in that sunny spot on the drive, too lazy to even twitch an ear.

"I rushed to clean everything up before you got home. Put his body in the back of the truck and ran away to hide it."

Rosco's body limp and dead. Tongue hanging out, blood on the gravel.

"Buried him on the back edge of Lenski's cornfield."

Travis stood, knocking his chair over. He turned into his room, shut the door, and slid to the floor, holding his head in his hands.

Rosco. Run over in his own driveway, just because Travis was too selfish to take him to the swamp. Because he wanted to see the foxes. *Stay,* Travis had told him, and Rosco had stayed.

Ba-bam — the bedroom door vibrated, and Travis jumped, his hands flying off his ears.

"Get out here," said Grandpa. "No hiding. We're going to deal with this."

Travis stood up and threw the door open.

"You did it on purpose!" he yelled.

"I didn't!" Grandpa yelled back, his face boiling red. "I loved that old hound before you were even born."

Travis pushed past Grandpa, out to the front porch.

The wind was electric with threat, and lightning flickered. He pressed against the house, arms crossed over his chest, trying to get the pictures out of his head. A jagged bolt lit across the gray western sky, followed by a sharp crack of thunder. Hailstones dropped, popping off the sidewalk. The wind picked up, blowing hail and rain onto the porch. Grandpa opened the door.

"Come in here."

"No."

"You're half-dressed and barefoot."

Travis kept feeling the thump, the gravel, the blood. The mud lump rose in his throat, and he tried to swallow it.

"I'd never hurt Rosco," Grandpa said through the screen. "Rather run over myself."

Why couldn't he stop, just quit talking, stop it? When Travis grabbed the door handle, Grandpa stepped aside and let him pass. He went directly to his room to get a shirt. Grandpa followed, standing in the doorway.

"Stormed like this the night your mama got sick. They left you alone in the house when they went to the hospital. Called me to babysit, said you were sound asleep."

Travis grabbed a pair of socks, sat on the edge of the bed, and pulled them on. He had to get out of there, storm or not.

"You weren't in your bed when I got there. Rosco found you hiding in your mama's closet. You latched right on to him. Squeezed his big long ear, and he didn't yipe or say a word. From that day on, he was your dog, not mine. You think I'd take that away from you? What kind of sonuvabitch do you think I am?"

Every word felt like a punch to Travis's chest, opening up the places he kept sealed off and secret. He couldn't remember the things Grandpa was saying, but he could feel them. He yanked his shoes on.

"When I hear you whimpering in your sleep, it always reminds me of that night."

Travis grabbed a sweatshirt and slammed through the kitchen and out the front door. The second he got outside, the mud ball in his throat broke loose for the first time in years. The hail had turned to rain, and he walked into it, fast and hard. The water from the sky mixed with the water on his face. The raindrops dove into puddles like bullets.

In that dark closet, reaching out for Rosco, the only thing he had. . . . Only Rosco wasn't there. Travis almost doubled over with the pain of it, sobs jerking him so hard he could barely walk.

He stopped at the bridge and grabbed the railing. His breath shook its way in, raggedy, and came out in sobs. The rain pulled, heavy and cold, on his sweatshirt. A passing car sprayed up water, soaking him from behind. He shivered as the cold crawled under his clothes, under his skin, all the way inside. He gulped in a bite of air, and another, but he couldn't stop the sobbing. He leaned over the water, hair dripping in his face.

Finally his chest stopped heaving. That was almost worse. Hollow and freezing cold. He hurried through town and into the school building, sloshing in his shoes. Down the stairs to the locker room. He landed on a bench and dropped his head into his hands. The tears rolled again, and his whole body shook with each breath. Those long soft ears. They felt like safe. Like not alone. *Th-thud,* blood. Did Grandpa run over his head?

He shivered harder.

"Travis?"

He almost jumped out of his goose-bumped skin.

"Are you okay?"

Bradley sat on a roll of wrestling mats in the corner by the showers. Travis hadn't even looked that way when he'd walked in, never thought anyone would be there so early. He wiped his hand over his face.

"Fine."

He cleared his throat to cover the quaver in his voice and pulled his sweatshirt over his head. It sucked and clung to him, hard to get off. If only he could hide in there forever. He took it into the shower area and wrung it out, his hands still shaking. He dumped the water out of his shoes, took off his socks, and wrung those, too.

"Here." Bradley appeared in the entryway with a towel. "You can use this."

Travis took the towel and rubbed his hair dry, wishing Bradley would go away. When he finally pulled the towel away from his face, Bradley was perched back on the wrestling mats. Travis took off his clammy T-shirt, full of cold rain and heat from his skin. He scrubbed the towel over his arms and back and chest, trying to rub in some warmth.

He wrung the T-shirt as dry as he could get it, and then pulled it back on. That made him cold all over again. His jeans were still dripping. He pulled on his wet socks and forced his feet into his shoes. He dried his face one more time and came out of the shower, tossing the towel to Bradley.

"You okay?" Bradley asked again.

Bradley had seen him sitting on the bench, must have heard those chokey noises coughing up his throat. Knew he'd been crying. Travis glanced at the clock.

"You look like you swam here," said Bradley.

Travis turned up one corner of his mouth and shrugged, the closest he could get to saying thanks. He left the locker room and ran upstairs to McQueen's office.

"Not an umbrella user, Mr. Roberts?" McQueen said when he showed up in the doorway.

"No, and I forgot to bring the book." Another cold shudder ran through him.

"How far do you live from here?"

"Not far."

"Here — here's a tardy pass." McQueen scribbled on a pad. "Go home and get some dry clothes on. You can't sit in school like that. We'll work on *Haunt Fox* fourth period. You won't miss anything."

Velveeta on WEDNESDAY

It's lunchtime and I'm in the girls' bathroom. Everything sucks so bad. This morning I checked Calvin's doorknob and it's locked and me with no key. My scarves are in there. What if I can't get them back?

I walked to school in the pouring-down rain. First person I saw was Bradley. He held up this little sign in front of his face: SAY YES. At first I couldn't figure out what it meant, but then I remembered about the stupid dance. I will not be saying yes.

Travis was absent. What if he really does have leukemia and now he's dying? What if our fight in the library pushed away his will to live?

Fourth period, I met with McQueen. I asked him how Travis was doing, and he said it was none of my business. Can you believe that? He one-trick-ponied me into helping and then says it's not my business and we're here to talk about me, not Travis, and Travis is turning his life around and what about me? He said, "Word on the street is you're not doing any homework." I told him we don't have streets in Russet. We only have roads. Then his social-worker starey eyes pounded me into a corner, and he said it's time to decide while I still have choices and I lose a choice or two every day I don't do homework.

I told him my only choices are which bar I waitress at.

He asked if I was trying to make that be so.

Chapter Twenty

By the time Travis passed the farm where Grandpa had stopped him on the first day of school, the sun peeked between the layers of gray, and a cool breeze had come up. His hair was almost dry, but his feet were still soggy. McQueen's tardy pass was soaked in the pocket of his wet jeans.

Lenski's cornfield. He should be able to get there before nightfall. It'd be easier if he had some water. Or money, so he could buy something when he passed through Salisbury. His stomach was hollow, and his mouth dry.

The sun climbed the layers of clouds, and big holes of blue opened in the sky. Travis peeled off his damp sweatshirt and tied it around his waist. A couple of potato trucks passed, loaded to the top. He'd just crossed the county line when the pickup pulled over on the opposite shoulder.

"Get in," Grandpa called out the window.

Travis kept walking.

"You've got maybe fourteen miles to go. Give or take. And you'll never find it if I don't show you. Get in."

Grandpa puttered along in the gravel, matching his speed.

"God, you're a stubborn shit."

He stopped, got out, slammed the truck door, and crossed the road. He didn't light up. He just walked alongside, keeping pace, even though Travis was going at a good clip.

"Look, I know I knocked you off your pins this morning. I'm sorry."

Travis had never heard those words out of Grandpa's mouth.

"Get in the truck and I'll take you there, right now."

Travis's feet hurt, especially his right heel. He felt like the skin might rot off if he didn't get it dry.

"Please? Get in the truck? I brought a sandwich along in case I found you."

Please? He'd never heard that word before, either. Travis made a sharp right, cutting Grandpa off. He crossed the road and walked back toward the truck. The lighter flicked behind him as Grandpa lit up. Travis got in the truck, took off his shoes, and peeled off his wet socks. The muscles in his legs twitched and quivered.

Grandpa came along, walking slowly now, dragging on his cigarette. Finally he got in and started the engine without a word. Travis grabbed the peanut-butter sandwich. Rammed it down and wished for some water, but not enough to say anything out loud. No sound in the truck but the tires on the road and sometimes the blinker.

Everything sparkled from the rain. That storm had washed out the last of summer, and now it was really fall. The leaves showed patches and runs of color. Sharp reds and bright yellows, breathing through the green.

The roads started to turn familiar, the ones Travis had ridden on the school bus for eight years. A couple of miles from the old place, Grandpa turned onto a dirt two-track with a line of trees on one side and a cornfield on the other. The corn had been cut, and the chopped-off stalks poked up out of the dirt, stretching in a wide pattern of yellow and brown. All dead. Grandpa stopped the truck.

"Look," he said. "You know I loved that hound, right? You don't really think I did that on purpose."

One time when Travis got up in the night, Grandpa had been sitting on the floor with his arms around Rosco, saying how much he loved him. He was sloppy drunk, but still. He never said that to Travis, drunk or sober. And as much as Rosco had loved Travis, it was Grandpa he obeyed.

Travis put his shoes back on with no socks, pulled on his sweatshirt, and got out of the truck. The birch and aspen alongside the field were on their way to yellow, and the patch of sumac had gone completely red. The leaves rustled and rattled in the wind.

"There's the spot." Grandpa pointed.

The dirt was still in clods, not settled. No grass growing. A big rock sat in the middle of the fresh dirt. Big enough that Travis wasn't sure he could lift it. Must have been hard for Grandpa to move.

Travis walked over to the grave.

"You want some time alone here?" asked Grandpa.

He nodded, and Grandpa got in the truck and backed out the two-track. Travis didn't have any more tears in him, just the big empty hole. Somewhere under the rock and the dirt were those long, soft ears. Travis used to put them across his face, the way Velveeta did with her scarves. He missed the smell, the dog hair on his clothes, and Rosco's deep *row-wow* bark. Most of all, he missed the way Rosco acted every day when he got home. Like nothing better in the world than Travis Roberts could come out of that school bus.

He knelt down and drew in the dirt. He outlined a hound like the one at the beginning of chapter two.

"I miss you, buddy," he said. "So much."

He'd been there just long enough to get chilly when the truck came bouncing back. The sad was all over Travis, inside and out, and it drowned out any mad he had left. Grandpa came over and sat down on the other side of the grave.

"Funny how this goose egg makes me feel better," he said after a while, touching his jaw. "Guess I felt like I needed to be whupped for what I did. I thought you were going to do it that day on the steps."

"I didn't touch you that day."

"Maybe not, but it felt that way. Lying there in the dirt, I had that AA moment-of-clarity thing. The one where you know the jig is up. Quitting time."

So that was it. That's why everything started changing that day. AA meetings and moving. If Travis had known Rosco was dead, the moving would have been different. If he'd known Grandpa did it . . . Well, who knows?

"It's harder than I thought," said Grandpa. "I figured once I detoxed, it'd be cake, but then it got harder in a different way. Guess I started feeling sorry for myself, and that's poison in the head. I'd be drinking now if you hadn't clobbered me."

"That's not why I did it," said Travis.

"I know. Doesn't matter. Same result. Travis, I swear to Christ Jesus I want to do right by you. Better than I did with your dad, anyway."

Grandpa's face sagged into tired wrinkles. Like an upside-down clown face.

"Did he drive into that tree on purpose?" Travis asked.

"I don't know. I've asked myself that a few times."

"Because of me?"

"Good God, is that what you think?" said Grandpa. "You're the only thing that mattered to him after your mama died. Never saw anyone love a kid like he loved you."

"Not enough to stay."

The words hung out there, vibrating. The breeze came through and knocked a few yellow leaves down.

"It's not that," said Grandpa finally. "The booze had him by the throat, same as me. It twists everything. Makes it all somebody else's fault."

Travis rolled a sharp pebble against his thumb, pressing hard so it hurt.

"Rosco's my fault," he said. "If I'd taken him, he wouldn't be dead."

"No!" Grandpa barked. "Shut up with that. Not your fault."

Travis rolled the pebble harder, making a dent-trail in his skin.

"This is, though." Grandpa tapped his chin. "Lucky I don't have a glass jaw, or you'd've shattered me all over the kitchen floor. You can't go around hitting people like that."

"I know," said Travis.

"I mean, if you have to, it's okay. But you can't just do it because you feel like it."

"I *know*."

Travis poked the pebble into the dirt on the edge of the

grave, pressing it in deep. The wind came colder through the cornstalks, and the sun dipped behind a cloud.

"Okay." Grandpa pushed himself up. "I gotta move before my knees rust so bad I can't get up again."

Travis waited until Grandpa was in the truck with the door closed. He ran his palm across the grave, smoothing over the hound drawing and the pebble hole. Then he stood and walked back to the truck. He hunched against the wind, his hands jammed in his pockets. Rosco was under there, under the dirt. Never coming back.

Everything was different now.

Velveeta Banished on WEDNESDAY

After school I told Connie about getting banished, and the way she looked at me, my eyes got wet. Especially when I told her my scarves were in there. She handed me a Kleenex and said I should ask for them and maybe I could apologize for trespassing.

I told her Sylvia would kill me and stuff my body in a rental truck, and then she'd have to get a new library lackey.

On the way home, I practiced saying I was sorry and please give me the scarves.

Sylvia opened the door just as I put my foot on the bottom step, and everything I'd practiced saying melted out of my brain. I just stood there on the doorstep half chokey and pathetic. I thought I might throw up. She stepped back and told me to come in. I didn't want to, but I wanted the scarves.

We stood there toe-to-toe in your kitchen and she started slugging lawyer questions at me like we were in a courtroom, only there wasn't anyone on my side to object.

HER: What did you have to do with my father?

me: He kind of watched out for me.

HER: He was your babysitter?

me: Nobody paid him.

HER: Did you know he had a daughter?

me: Yes.

HER: What did he say about me?

me: That he was a bad dad and you won't forgive him for it.

HER: He said that?

me: More than once.

HER: He was.

me: Not to me.

She almost rocked over backward when I said that, like I'd smacked her hard. But she came back with her voice slicey-sharp.

HER: I think you should go now. Where do you live?

me: Next door. I come here sometimes because I miss him.

She leaned against the wall then, staring at me. I stared back. I figured if it was a stare-down, I'm good at that. I stared and she stared and neither of us blinked for a long time.

HER: What is it that you want from me?

me: I want the scarves. He gave them to me — they're mine.

HER: Why would he give you my mother's scarves?

I stared at her without any words like I was Travis. She turned her back on me and looked out the window like I wasn't worth beating in a stare-down.

HER: Go home.

me: What about my scarves?

HER: He didn't put anything in writing. You could be lying for all I know.

me: But I'm not. He was right when he said you've got a mean streak.

HER: Get out of here before I call the cops.

I hate her.

Chapter Twenty-one

A few kids were scattered around the lunchroom, eating breakfast, but Velveeta wasn't there. Travis wandered past her locker a few times. Maybe she was still mad at him for walking out on her at the library Monday. That seemed so long ago now.

She didn't show up first period, either. Where could she be? Something must be wrong. He kept *Haunt Fox* tucked inside one of his textbooks and worked on it all morning. He went over and over the words he knew and circled the unknown ones farther ahead.

"Hey, Travis." Bradley came up behind him in the lunch line. "Where's Velveeta?"

"How should I know?" Travis pulled away. "Ask her yourself."

"I can't — she's not here."

Travis got his food and sat at the usual table, kitty-corner from Amber and her book. He pulled out *Haunt Fox*. Amber's eyes roved back and forth over her pages quickly, and she flipped a page. Travis tried to move his eyes fast over the first line, but he lost words.

He was headed back to his locker after lunch when Chad Cormick shouldered up next to him.

"Hey, Roberts, want to fight me?" he asked.

He nudged Travis, then danced back, both fists up, grinning.

"No."

"Yeah, you do. Come on, show me how it's done."

He tapped Travis on the shoulder again, fake-punched toward his head, and kept his feet dancing. Travis turned away, and Chad danced around in front of him.

"Come on, dude! Why you gotta be so like that?" He pointed at his chin. "Right here, come on, just one."

Travis shifted the book to his left hand, brought his fist up, and dinked Chad on the jaw. Hard, but not mean. Chad twirled, fell to the floor, and popped back up.

"Check it — you didn't even put your book down to deck me. Roberts, you are the moolio."

He lightly slapped Travis on the side of the head,

hopped backward, and spun away. Like a fox puppy, bouncing down the hall. Velveeta would have loved that. Where was she, anyway?

After the last bell, Travis poked his head into Room 134. Grandpa had gotten a letter from school about parent-teacher conferences. He'd never gone to one before, but he'd been talking as if he might actually do it.

"What's on your mind?" asked McQueen.

"What do you tell parents at conferences?"

"We go over your work and your grades on assignments and talk about any problems or anything that's going especially well. Why? Is there something you do or don't want me to tell your parents?"

"My grandpa," said Travis. "If he comes. He might not. But if he does. He doesn't know, you know."

"Doesn't know you have trouble reading?"

"Not exactly."

"And you don't want him to know?" McQueen raised his eyebrows to the ceiling.

"Well, I want him to know I'm doing good. If he comes."

"I'll tell him you're doing well, that you're one of my best students. I won't go into specific detail about the work unless he asks. But if he asks, I'll answer every question honestly. How's that?"

"That's good."

Travis pushed out the double doors and into the cold breeze. *One of my best students.* The sky was sunny-sharp blue, and leaves skittered along the sidewalk. A good day to lie on the merry-go-round and watch the trees spin. Travis headed for the park but stopped short in the alley.

Hard, mean laughter smacked out from a huddle by the slide. He flattened against the building and peeked around the corner. Three of the guys from the picnic table had Bradley backed against the ladder. The tall guy with long dark hair—Maddox?—laughed again. Chilson said something in a low voice, and Travis caught a glimpse of Bradley's face. He was scared half to death, actually crying.

He'd been nice to Travis in the locker room, didn't even say a word about it later. And anyway, three on one was too much for anyone. Especially Bradley. Travis dropped his backpack off of his shoulder and pushed away from the building.

"Whistler!" he yelled.

"Look, Chilson," said Maddox. "It's Skinnyboy from the bridge! What you want, Skinnyboy?"

Travis pushed through and grabbed Bradley by the front of his jacket, jerking him away from the slide. Bradley was so startled, he almost fell over, but Travis hauled him upright and gave him a hard shove.

"Did you think I was kidding?" yelled Travis. "Pay up or I'll kill you."

"Oh, look," said Chilson. "Bradley's popular today. What do you want with him, Skinnyboy?"

"None of your business," said Travis.

"Ooooo." Maddox took a step back with his hands in the air. "Tough guy."

The short guy in the monster-truck T-shirt laughed. Travis grabbed Bradley again by the collar and yanked him, making space between them and the three guys. He started walking fast toward the bleachers, dragging Bradley with him.

"Don't cry, Bradley!" called Maddox. "Don't cry! Boo-hoo-hoo, Bradley!"

Travis pulled Bradley up past the back of the tavern toward Main Street, and let him go as soon as they were out of sight. Bradley crumpled on the ground next to the building.

"Bradley, get up. They might follow us."

Travis stepped to the corner of the building and looked back at the playground. Monster Truck had found Travis's backpack by the building. He opened it and pulled out *Haunt Fox*. Travis turned to Bradley.

"Stay there," he said.

That guy had his book. If he opened it, he'd see the pencil marks. What if he ripped it up? *You can't go around hitting people.* Grandpa's voice spoke in his head as he stomped back across the park.

Chilson spotted Travis and grinned. Monster Truck tossed the book on the ground.

"Hey, Skinnyboy," said Chilson. "You think I'm stupid? You think I fell for that?"

Travis stopped about five feet away. Maddox and Monster Truck moved up, one on each side. Travis took a couple of steps back so he could watch all three of them.

"What do you want?" asked Chilson. "You saved your girlfriend. Now, get out of here before we kick your skinny ass."

If Travis looked at the book — if they knew how much he wanted it — he'd never get it back.

"Why pick on Bradley?" he asked. "He's like half your size."

"Point." Chilson nodded. "But you're not. So you think you can take all three of us?"

Travis looked them over, one at a time, then centered back on Chilson.

"Probably not. But maybe."

"You think you're pretty tough, huh?" said Maddox.

He stepped in, chesting up close. Travis knocked him back. He shoved, and Travis shoved harder. Maddox stumbled and almost went down. Travis's hands came up into fists, and he felt the heat moving through him, pumping but not boiling over. Maddox bounced back, and Travis zeroed in, gauging the distance between them.

"Hey, look," said Chilson. "There's Bradleycakes. I guess he's going to save you."

"Shit," said Monster Truck. "He's on his phone."

Travis didn't turn to look. He kept his eyes nailed on Maddox, who was moving in.

"You know what, Skinnyboy?" Chilson shouldered between them. He pointed his finger at Travis's nose. "I like you. You've got guts."

"I'll stomp his guts," said Maddox.

"Not now," said Chilson. He turned and left through the alley, and Monster Truck followed.

"I'll see you later," Maddox said, glaring at Travis. He held up both middle fingers as he backed away. "Count on it."

Travis waited until they'd all turned the corner, then picked up *Haunt Fox* and put it in his backpack.

"I'm sorry," said Bradley, coming up behind. "I should have backed you up right away. I just—"

"Don't worry about it. The phone was smart. Did you really call anyone?"

Bradley shook his head and slumped slowly to the ground. "I hate them," he said, his hands over his face. "I really hate them."

Travis was still juiced from the almost fight. Grabbing Bradley by the shirt, shoving him around . . . he'd actually enjoyed that part a little bit. Even if it was to keep him from getting killed.

Bradley kept talking, shaky-voiced, heaving words as if he couldn't get them out fast enough.

"We were sort of friends, Josh and me, when we were little. Then he started picking on me. Last year, when he was still in middle school, I was scared to go in the bathroom even."

Travis stopped pacing and sat on the edge of the merry-go-round. He leaned over and picked up a couple of rocks.

"And when you came up, they were saying all the stuff

they're going to do to me and . . . If you wouldn't have showed up, Travis . . ."

Bradley tried to suck in a sob, but it got loose and then he couldn't quit. Travis had never seen anyone cry that hard before, nobody but himself on the bridge. The cold wind blew through, and Travis shivered. He wanted to leave before those guys came back, but he couldn't leave Bradley crying alone in the dirt.

"Hey, it's okay," he said. "Really, come on."

Bradley's whole body shook and jerked so hard that Travis felt it himself, deep in his chest. Finally, Bradley slowed down and took a big shaky breath. He scrubbed his face with the back of his hand and turned to Travis.

"You're going to hate me now, too."

"Nope," said Travis. "Not for that."

"Why do I have to be so scared?"

"Everybody's scared of something."

"You're just saying that to make me feel better."

"No, I'm not."

Bradley stared until Travis looked away.

"You really are like the Master Chief," he said. "You neutralized all three of them just because I'm on your squad. Aren't you scared of them at all?"

"A little." Travis shrugged. "Three on one, that's something to watch out for."

"I've never been in a fight. But you didn't even hit anybody — they just backed off."

That was true. Travis hadn't hit anybody. He'd just

growled like Larry the dog. No concussions, nobody on the ground, no cold sludge in his guts.

"Come on," he said. "I'll walk you as far as the bridge in case they're still hanging around."

They walked in silence until they got in sight of the bridge. The picnic table was empty.

"I lied when I told Velveeta I don't lie," said Bradley. "I lie all the time to my dad. I leave early for school so I won't run into those guys and I say it's to study. That's why I was in the locker room yesterday morning. I say I have chess club after school, but really I stay in the school library or wait in the park until they leave the picnic table."

"Geez, Bradley," said Travis.

"I'm un-asking Velveeta to the dance. You should ask her. She likes you better. Are you scared to ask her? Is that what you're scared of?"

Travis shrugged.

"It's okay. I won't tell."

Velveeta on THURSDAY

I've been wearing the same scarf for four days in a row. It's my only one now and forever. If I knew I could only have one, I would have kept that orange one.

Walking toward school, I thought about no scarves and no trailer, never again.

When I got to the library, my feet turned. They took me to the back door, and I sat there on the cold cement, freezing, until Connie showed up. She let me in, even though the library doesn't open until ten. I told her about Sylvia not giving me the scarves, and then I started crying and couldn't stop. Connie hugged me. Nobody ever touches me anymore. Not even a pat on the shoulder. That made me cry harder.

Connie got me some Kleenex and asked if I was ready to go to school, and I told her if I went there, I'd puke. She asked if I'd eaten anything and I said no. After some hemming and hawing, she said I could spend the day at the library, but I couldn't just sit there — did I have any homework?

I pulled out *The Book Thief,* and Connie got this funny squint-eyed look on her face, kind of like someone was stabbing her and telling her a joke at the same time. She asked me how far I was, and I told her I was almost done but it was too depressing to finish. The girl Liesel already learned how to read, and now everything is about war and people dying. Connie said I could stay at the library all day if I finished the book. I told her she is in cahoots with McQueen and that's probably illegal, but she pointed at the book and said she'd be back before ten, and locked the door on her way out.

She came back with scones and muffins from the bakery and sent me to the study room to keep reading. I couldn't eat because that book made me cry so hard, I couldn't even breathe. Connie said to keep reading and keep breathing, like that was easy. Tears and snot just about came out of my butt, I cried so hard. After I finished the book, Connie fixed up a spot in the study room with a pillow.

I told her that Calvin being dead is like a long-fingered claw that keeps scratching at my heart. She said she knows that claw. She said grief is a rough ride but the only way through it is through it. Then she told me to take a nap.

Liesel the book thief was tough.

I'm not tough.

I'm not anything.

Chapter Twenty-two

Travis high-low whistled, and Larry came barking down the driveway. Travis threw him half a muffin.

"Hey, Larry. Didn't know if you'd be out this early on a cold morning."

The rising sun touched the frost tipping the grass and weeds, painting a frigid sparkle picture. Larry swallowed the muffin and came closer. Travis knelt on the driveway, holding out his hand, palm up.

"Come on, Lar. It's okay. Look, I even know your name now."

"How do you know his name?"

Travis jumped to his feet. Larry turned and ran back to the old woman. She leaned on her cane and looked down at Larry, who now sat in front of her.

"How does this boy know your name, Larry?"

"I heard you call him that one day." He turned around, walking quickly back to the road. "I'm leaving."

"This boy heard me call your name?" The woman talked louder, so Travis would hear. "I wonder where he heard that? I've never seen him before. And Larry, it looks like you're friends with him. You let him walk right up the drive. I wonder why you did that."

"It's not his fault." Travis turned around to face her. "I gave him some baloney."

"Bribed! By a boy with baloney."

"Sorry, I won't do it again."

"Larry, I wonder if this boy would want to take you for a walk sometime. I bet you'd both like that."

"He wouldn't go with me. I tried."

"Since this boy is not afraid of you and seems to feel free to wander around our driveway, maybe he would come up to the house sometime. Maybe he'd knock on the door and introduce himself."

Larry wagged his tail. If Travis had one, he might have twitched the end of it.

"Okay, then, let's hope he does that. But right now, I think the boy should go to school and we should go indoors. It's cold out here."

She started back up the drive, Larry next to her. Travis watched until they went around the curve and out of sight. Then he hurried to school so he wouldn't be late for McQueen.

"Before we get started," McQueen said, "I want to check in with you again about your other classes. I've mentioned to your other teachers that you're working with me—"

"Did you tell them?" Travis's head snapped up.

"Mr. Roberts"—McQueen's voice dropped so low, Travis leaned forward to hear him—"do you think they don't know? You never turn anything in, you don't do class projects, and math is the only class where you participate at all."

The skin on Travis's neck started the slow burn upward.

"If you'd kept pretending with me, you wouldn't be rattling off lists of words now," said McQueen. "You need to talk to your teachers. And start paying attention in the classroom."

Travis couldn't pay attention. *Haunt Fox* and word lists were all he could handle.

"Don't worry so much. Might be more slack lying around for you than you know. Ask Ms. Gordon about that reading program. Plenty of kids with vision or reading problems use it. Now, let's see, I think we were starting chapter two, weren't we?"

McQueen started reading about a boy and his hound puppy who found the fox's tracks. Travis let himself fall inside the story and forget about everything else. The boy headed out in the new snow to follow his hound and the fox.

"So, how are the words going?" McQueen closed the book.

"I need a new list. And I've circled all the way through chapter four."

McQueen wrote down a new list of five words, and they went over them a few times.

"You know quite a few words now, and you've got some uncircled space to run in," said McQueen. "I'd like you to start looking at a sentence or two, where you know all the words. Read them out loud, and take it slow. When you hit a comma, stop and chew. When you hit a period, swallow. Don't try to eat any circled words."

"Only the ones that go down easy?"

"Right." McQueen grinned. "I don't want you gagging. Now, go on — the first bell's about to ring."

Travis stopped in the doorway to Ms. Gordon's room. Velveeta was there in her seat, watching the door. She smiled. A soft, close-lipped smile. Relief whooshed over Travis as he sat in front of her.

"Where've you been?" he asked.

"I was here Wednesday — where were you? I thought maybe you had the bubonic plague."

"So were you sick those other days or having Velveeta time?"

"Neither."

Bradley popped up at Travis's locker before fourth period.

"Hey, I un-asked Velveeta to the dance," he said. "Plus I told my dad about what happened in the park. He said to invite you over. Want to come home with me after school tonight?"

"What did she say?" They walked into McQueen's room.

"She who?"

"Velveeta. About the dance."

"She doesn't care. She didn't want to go with me anyway. So what about tonight?"

"Mr. Whistler," said McQueen. "Seat, please."

Travis pulled out *Haunt Fox,* but he couldn't concentrate. Every time he looked over at Velveeta, she was staring straight ahead at nothing. Then McQueen called her into his office and she was in there for a long time. When she came out, she put her head down on her desk. The bell rang and she didn't move. Travis started to walk over and see if she was okay, and then he stopped. Took another step forward. Then another one back. Finally he backed out of the room and got in line for lunch.

When he came out with his lunch tray, she was sitting with Bradley. He waved, and Travis sat across from them. Velveeta didn't have any lunch in front of her.

"Hey, Travis. I told her about yesterday," said Bradley.

"He says you neutralized Chilson and his buddies," said Velveeta. "I'm not really sure what that means, but it sounds impressive. Better than me. I got dumped by Bradley Whistler."

"No, you didn't! You didn't want to go with me."

"Aren't I supposed to decide that?"

"No," said Bradley. "I asked you. I can un-ask you."

Travis chewed through a taco, listening and watching. Velveeta said Velveeta-like things, but she said them with the volume turned down and the lights dim. As if she was running on half-power.

"It doesn't really bother you, does it?" asked Bradley. "That I un-asked you? I mean, it seems like something is bothering you."

Travis caught Velveeta's eye, and she quickly looked away. As if she didn't want anyone seeing her.

"Bradley," said Travis, "do that 'what's the password?' thing you do."

Velveeta looked sideways at Travis with one tiny nod. Thanking him.

"Really? Right now?"

"Yeah, come on," said Travis. "Do it."

Bradley launched in, knocking on the table. "'Hey, open up.' 'What's the password?' 'Password? Oh, man, I forgot.'"

Bradley kept going, and Travis set his whole chocolate-chip cookie on a napkin and slid it in front of Velveeta. She met his eyes, but he could barely see her. She was way back there. Hiding.

"I've got chicken stir-fry," said Bradley, breaking out of his password rap. "You want some, Velveeta?"

"I'm not hungry." She pushed Travis's cookie back. "But thanks, anyway. I'll see you later."

She left, even though there was still more than five minutes until the bell.

"Something really is wrong, isn't it?" Bradley asked. "Do you think she's waiting for you to ask her to the dance?"

Velveeta walked across the lunchroom, her head down. Like the day he'd hurt her in the hallway, only ten times more. Whatever was wrong, it was bigger than anything Travis knew about.

Velveeta on FRIDAY

Bradley un-asked me to the dance as soon as I got to school. Whatever.

McQueen dragged me into his office. I gave *The Book Thief* back. He asked me a bunch of questions, I guess to make sure I'd really read the whole thing. He said he didn't make me read it because of Travis.

I told him not to lie, and he said helping Travis was only a tiny part of it. Then he said to relax and put my feet up because he was going to read me his favorite part. So I put my feet on the stack of books in front of his desk. He read the part about Death coming for Liesel's papa.

That's the part that made tears come out of my butt. Liesel's papa reminds me too much of Calvin. I couldn't figure out how McQueen knew, and I was thinking maybe Connie told him. I was starting to get mad about that when he slammed the book shut and pointed at me and said "That's you." "That's me what?" I asked him.

Then he got all *Stand and Deliver*ish and said I was that kind of person, the kind who sits up when Death comes to get them. The souls who put out a lot of light in the world. Like Liesel's papa. Like Liesel.

I told him I am not like Liesel at all. My voice shook like crazy, just like I was one of the kids in that movie.

And McQueen said yes, I am. He said I'm one of the best

sitter-uppers he's ever met, and that's why he gave me *The Book Thief* to read.

Then he just sat there and stared at me, and that was good because it made me settle down. I was not going to get eye-wet in front of those snakey social-worker eyes. He gave me a little teeny-tiny smile like he knew that, and then he waved at the door and told me to get out of there.

All I can think about is Calvin dying. Did he sit up when Death came, like Liesel did? Did he look Death in the eye? Was he sad about leaving? Does he miss me? Because I miss him so much I can't stand it. It's like my heart is getting pulverized with a sharp-pointed jackhammer, every second and all the time.

When I got home from school, I checked his trailer door, just in case.

Locked.

Chapter Twenty-three

Saturday morning, Travis leaned on the bridge railing and looked out over the pond. Beneath his feet the water ran and rumbled over the dam. Out ahead it lay flat and still, reflecting the trees in a perfect upside-down image. He looked down Water Street toward Bradley's house.

He'd gone there after school and met Bradley's mom. She was nice. So was his dad. But what about Velveeta? He didn't know anything about her outside of school, not one single thing, except that she watched a lot of movies, she worked at the library, and she did her own laundry. If she was sick, who took care of her? Someone like Grandpa? Or someone like Bradley's parents? Or nobody at all? Did she have brothers and sisters? A dog?

Travis headed down the street to the bakery. Grandpa liked working there, and not just for the doughnuts. He said it did him good. Travis had never been in there, had never even walked on that side of the street. The sign, *Harvest Moon Bakery*, hung out from the front of the building like a flag.

He pushed the screen door open, ringing the bell overhead. Grandpa turned from the coffee machine, and his mouth actually dropped open.

"Hey," said Travis. "Can I get half a dozen doughnut holes?"

"Yessir." Grandpa grinned as if Travis had just given him a big present wrapped up with a shiny bow. He opened the display case, pulled them out with tongs, and dropped them in a paper bag. "What's this for? You don't like doughnuts, remember?"

"Feed the birds."

Grandpa looked him up and down, slit-eyed.

"Pretty expensive way to feed the birds." He rang it up on the cash register. "Dollar fifty."

Travis paid with the spare change Grandpa always left lying on the coffee table, and put an extra quarter in the tip jar. Grandpa stared at it, then back at Travis, and broke into a cackle.

"You crack me up, boy," he said. "Go feed the birds."

The bakery bell rang behind Travis as he turned onto the sidewalk. A sparrow chirped from the bushes, asking for its handout, and he rolled the top of the bag tighter. A squirrel made a dash across the street. The closer Travis got to the library, the slower he walked.

Maybe she didn't want him coming there. Maybe he'd be bugging her. Maybe whatever was wrong was none of his business. He stood in the library entryway and looked through the window. The angles were all wrong; he couldn't see anything but books. Finally, he opened the door.

"Hi, Travis." Connie looked up from the computer at the front desk. "Velveeta's busy right now, but have a seat and she'll come find you."

Travis took out his math book and started in on the homework. He'd talked to Mrs. Lane on Friday afternoon and said he had trouble with the story problems. She'd been much nicer than he expected.

"What's that, math?" whispered Velveeta. She pulled a chair up next to him. "Why are you doing that?"

"I brought you something." He handed her the bakery bag.

"What is this?" She looked inside. "Nice. But I can't eat them now or I'll get fired."

She took the bakery bag into a back room and shut the door. Connie, who was watching from the front desk, smiled at Travis and nodded. Not like she was mad at Velveeta for slacking off. More like she and Travis were in on some secret together.

He kept working on the math, looking ahead to see if he could figure things out on his own. Velveeta came back over at noon and sat across from him.

"Why are you still here?" she asked.

"Waiting for you. What are you doing now?"

"Taking my laundry home. What are you doing?"

"Helping you?"

Velveeta's mouth turned down. Like she was mad.

"I gotta check with Connie about something."

She and Connie disappeared in back for almost fifteen minutes. Travis figured he'd done something wrong, but he had no idea what it was. Finally, the door to the study room opened, and Velveeta nodded. He picked up his books and followed her. He glanced at Connie on the way, and she gave him two thumbs up. Whatever that meant.

"So, Travis, why are you here, really?" Velveeta retrieved her red wagon from behind the library. She put the bakery bag beneath a towel.

"I don't know — to cheer you up, I guess." He reached for the handle of the wagon. "Seems like something's wrong."

"I can pull my own wagon." She pushed his hand away. "What makes you think something's wrong?"

"For one thing, you're wearing the same scarf you wore yesterday."

Velveeta stopped dead in her tracks.

"I'm sorry," said Travis quickly. "I like this scarf — it's a good one — it's just that you usually don't . . ."

She started walking again. Travis walked next to her, kicking himself for saying anything about the scarf.

"How's the reading going?" Her voice sounded funny. Like she was choking on something.

"It's okay."

"Are you ever going to let me help you again?"

"You don't let *me* help *you*. You won't even let me pull your wagon."

The words flew out of his mouth. As if they came directly from his guts and forgot to pass his brain on the way. Velveeta stopped again. She dropped her head, and her hair fell forward so it hid her face. He waited, hoping she'd just give him the wagon handle.

"Don't follow me," she said.

She took off, the wagon rattling behind. Travis stood on the sidewalk and watched until she turned the corner. She didn't look back.

Velveeta on Saturday

I had to go ask Connie what to do when Travis brought me doughnut holes. I told her I didn't have it in me to make him laugh. I told her I'm the entertainment monkey and people only like me because I make them laugh.

She said, "Velveeta, honey, if that's the only thing you give them, then that's the only thing they're going to know to want."

She said Travis has the sweetest face she's ever seen and if he wants to be my friend, I should let him. But I don't know how. When he said I'd been wearing the same scarf every day, I felt like he was stabbing me in the guts, not in a mean way but like he could see inside of me whether I told him anything or not.

Then he said that thing about wanting to help me. How I wouldn't even let him pull my wagon.

I thought my heart was going to fall out of my chest — that's how bad it hurt.

Why did that hurt? It doesn't make any sense.

I don't understand anything.

CHAPTER TWENTY-FOUR

Velveeta was still wearing the green scarf first period on Monday. She waved the end of it at Travis when he walked in the door. Not mad.

"Thanks for the doughnut holes," she said. "You kept me from getting malnutritioned over the weekend."

"Are you okay?"

"I don't have the bubonic plague or a broken leg. So yup, I'm okay. Pay attention — the teacher's talking."

Travis faced front. She seemed more okay. Not one hundred percent, but definitely better. But why was she still wearing the same scarf?

"You know what you said?" she whispered, jabbing the back of his neck. "About how I won't let you help me? You help me all the time."

How, or when, had he ever helped Velveeta? She never needed help. She helped him, and all he'd ever done was hurt her, like that time in the hallway. Plus the time he'd told her to quit bugging him. That wasn't helping.

He snagged Bradley in the hallway before fourth period.

"Can you do me a favor?" he asked. "Don't sit by us at lunch, okay? I want to ask Velveeta about something."

"You going to ask her?" Bradley's eyes fired up. "About the dance?"

"Bradley, get off the dance. I just have to ask her something, and lunch is the only chance I'll get."

The smile fell off Bradley's face. He took a step back and looked Travis over like he was calculating a complicated equation.

"Something private?"

"Sort of," said Travis.

"Okay." Bradley nodded, his face serious. "I understand."

At lunchtime Velveeta said, "Hey, look — Bradley's sitting with Reed and Jake. Is he done with us already?"

"I told him to leave us alone today," said Travis.

"Why?"

"What did you mean this morning when you said I helped you?" He rushed the words before he chickened out. "How?"

Velveeta picked up the end of the green scarf and fingered the fringes. She squeezed them together in a ponytail and then spread them out.

"Helping you learn words is the best thing that happened to me in the last forty-four days," she said.

Travis counted back. Forty-four days — that would be sometime in August. Around the time they'd moved to Russet. Velveeta's pizza sat untouched on her plate.

"Did you ever have a place that was really good?" She talked down to her scarf. "Someplace you could go and everything was sort of more okay?"

"Yes," said Travis.

"Do you still go there?"

"No. We moved away from it."

The silence stretched. Travis finished his pizza.

"Do you have a place like that?" he asked.

"I did," said Velveeta. "Now I don't. All my scarves used to be there. Now I can't go to the place anymore, and all the scarves are gone except for this one."

Whatever she was saying and not saying, he could feel it all the way inside. It hurt. Velveeta kept staring at her scarf as the minutes ticked by.

"Are you going to eat your pizza?"

"No," she said. "You can have it if you want."

"I don't. Just seems like maybe you should eat something."

She looked up at him, and her eyes were the softest he'd ever seen them. She didn't smile, but she stretched her lips a bit.

"You're nice, Travis," she said. "Really, really nice."

The bell rang, and she got up. Travis followed, careful not to crowd her. She threw her whole lunch in the trash. Her pizza lay upside down on top of the other garbage.

That evening, Grandpa left for parent-teacher conferences at 7:35, and Travis paced the house from 7:36 until 7:49. Then he went out in the yard. The breeze ran goose bumps across his skin.

He traced the steps of the phantom dog around the inside of the fence. The last of the dog dookey had disintegrated. Travis paced the yard one way and then turned and circled in the other direction. What would McQueen say about him? What if Grandpa swore or lit up a cigarette in McQueen's office?

When headlights turned into the driveway, Travis ran back inside and jumped on the couch. He put his feet on the coffee table and grabbed the remote. The TV flicked on just as the front door opened.

"Hey, Trav."

Grandpa went into his room. Travis stared at the TV, holding his breath. Wasn't he going to say anything? After a few minutes, Grandpa came back out, picked up the remote, and clicked the TV off. He set something with a clink on the coffee table.

Rosco's collar. Beat-up brown leather, with the rabies tag still attached.

"You want that?" Grandpa lit a cigarette.

Travis picked it up, turning it over in his hands. The inside was greasy, the feel of Rosco still there.

"I should've given it to you a while ago, but. Well. I didn't." He kicked back the recliner and took a deep drag. "So this McQueen fellow, he's taken quite a shine to you."

"Yeah?" Travis's pulse thudded in his ears. "What'd he say?"

"Said he's never seen a kid try so hard. Said you've got an A in his class and you've been coming in early to do extra work."

Travis ran his fingers across the stitches in the old leather collar.

"And that Ms. Gordon—you have a D in her class right now, but she thinks you'll do better the second half of the quarter."

He cleared his throat, and Travis looked up. Grandpa cleared his throat another time and tapped the long ash of his cigarette into the ashtray.

"Trav," he said, "I know it doesn't help much now, but..."

"It's okay." Travis said it fast.

"I should've known."

Grandpa stubbed out his cigarette, closed his eyes,

and leaned his head back. He swallowed, his Adam's apple jerking up and down. Then he cleared his throat again and looked Travis in the eye.

"I've been keeping that collar in my room to remind me why I shouldn't drink. But I don't need it now. I look at you and I can remember pretty good."

Velveeta on MONDAY

I almost told Travis things about Trailer World today. Maybe he really is an undercover cop. Sometimes he says exactly the right thing and it almost cracks me open. I stopped by the library on my way home, and Connie gave me three DVDs. She said they came in as donations but they're duplicates and I can have them.

I said that's real nice, but thanks to Sylvia I don't have anything to watch them on.

One of them is *Running on Empty*. I love that movie. I remember the last time I saw it. Calvin made popcorn, and afterward he gave a big lecture about boys and staying out of trouble. I loved it when he lectured me.

When I got home tonight, the madre was freaking because Jimmy said he's moving to Texas. He has said that seventy-eight times before, so why would this time be different.

Tonight is parent-teacher conferences. The madre has never gone once. She says me and Jimmy got it backward, that he should be the smart one so he could make us millionaires and I could stay home and take care of her. Instead it's me that's smart and that just means I'm going to leave her and she'll be all alone.

I want her to be right about that, and I feel super-bad that I want her to be right about that.

If I leave her, will I turn out like Sylvia? Rich and mean?

Chapter Twenty-Five

Travis stopped in to see Ms. Gordon. She took him to the computer lab and showed him how to get into the shared files under her name.

"This file has your initials," she said. "I've scanned most of the material from the first few weeks in here."

She handed Travis the headphones. He put them on, and the computer started reading the text to him. Yellow shading jumped across the section being read, chewing through a word at a time. Ms. Gordon showed him how he could adjust speed, back up, and ask the computer to give him an out-loud definition if he didn't know a word.

"Stay here through first period this morning," she said, "and get the feel of it. Try different speeds. See here — you can make the text bigger or smaller, and you can take it a word at a time or a phrase at a time, whichever you like."

"So you can put any book on here?"

"We just have to scan it in. I'll show you how. You could ask your other teachers to put material on here, too."

He spent the rest of the hour playing with the Kurzweil. Speeding up, slowing down, watching the yellow highlighter crawl across the words. He made it read the same sentence over and over to see if he could mouth the words along with it.

The voice wasn't as good as McQueen's, not by a long shot. It was machiney and choppy. Good for reading textbooks, not fox stories. But it meant that he could read. Social studies. Science. All those handouts they gave him that he ditched in a folder. He could find out what they said. All of them.

"So, Travikins," said Velveeta when he sat down at lunch. "Bradley here tells me you've been walking home with him. Are you his official bodyguard now?"

"No." Travis looked at Bradley. "Did you tell her that?"

"She made the bodyguard part up. Next time I run into them, I'm going to try what you said." He turned to Velveeta. "Travis says if I treat them halfway normal, they'll leave me alone. Do you think that'll work?"

"Why'd you say that?" Velveeta asked Travis. "They'll kill him."

"Maybe, but when he acts all scared, it makes them want to kill him more. Like if you run away from a mean dog, it's going to chase you and kill you."

"Chilson, mean dog, grrr, bark, slobber, grr," said Bradley.

"He's not a dog," said Travis. "You say stuff like that, no wonder he doesn't like you."

"You're the one who said dog."

"I didn't say *he* was a dog."

"I didn't mean anything by it," said Bradley.

"Well, nobody really means anything by anything, do they, Bradley?" said Velveeta. "Travis has a point. Maybe Chilson thinks you think you're better than him."

"Maybe I am," said Bradley. "I'm smarter for sure."

Travis looked up and met Velveeta's eyes.

"Should I try to be not smart?" asked Bradley. "It's not my fault I'm smart and he's not."

"Yeah, but it's your fault you go around saying that," said Travis.

"Bradley." Velveeta stood up as the bell rang. "If you're really as smart as you think you are, you'd listen to Travis more."

As she walked away, Bradley grabbed Travis by the sleeve.

"Did you see how she looked at you?" he whispered. "She totally wants you."

"Bradley, shut up."

"Okay. But she does."

Travis sat in Life Skills sixth period, not listening. Velveeta's volume was still turned down. It had to be about her place and her scarves. Whatever happened, maybe it was as bad as his place and his dog. Maybe worse.

After the last bell, he walked alone through town, working over a new idea. He forgot all about the picnic table until he got to the bridge.

"Hey, Skinnyboy," yelled Chilson. "Where's Bradleycakes? Did you two break up?"

Just Chilson and Maddox were there. Travis reached in his pocket and found Rosco's rabies tag. He'd taken it off the collar and put it on his key ring the night before. He crossed the bridge and walked directly down the slope to the table. By the time he got there, Maddox was on his feet. Chilson stayed on the table, his feet on the bench.

"You want to stomp my guts now?" asked Travis.

He'd never walked into a fight on purpose before. They always just happened.

Maddox walked in a circle around him. "I kind of do," he said. "I'm not sure you're worth the trouble, though. Seems like a lot of work, making your guts spout out your nose."

"Can you guys just lay off of Bradley then?" Travis said to Chilson.

"Why should we?" Chilson flicked his butt away.

"You know you can make him cry — so what? What's it prove?"

"Ooo, that's all deep," said Maddox. "So now you're telling us what to do?"

"No." Travis said it to Chilson. "Just asking."

He turned and walked away. His back crawled with the hope and the dread of Maddox rushing up behind him, but it didn't happen. When he got up to the road, he turned and looked over his shoulder. Maddox was back on the picnic table. They both had new cigarettes lit.

Travis walked on up the hill, hammering away at his new idea. He turned it over and around, looking at it from every angle. It was risky. Much riskier than inviting Maddox to stomp his guts.

"Hey, Grandpa," he said when the front door opened. "How was your day?"

"What do you want?" Grandpa looked at him sideways.

"I was just wondering — I know someone else is renting the old place now, but what if I wanted to go back to the swamp? Just to walk around back there? Do you think they'd mind?"

"I could call Chuck and ask him to check with them," said Grandpa. "How you planning to get there?"

"I was hoping you might drop me and a friend there on Saturday when you get off work. I want to show her the swamp."

"Her? This friend is a her?"

"She's just a friend."

"What's her name, this just a friend?"

"Okay, forget it." Travis got off the couch. "If you're going to make it into a big thing, forget it."

He shut his bedroom door behind him and dropped onto the bed. What made him think for even a second that could work?

"Don't sulk!" yelled Grandpa through the door. "God, boy, you are the touchiest thing crawling. Can't you take a joke?"

"No!"

The TV came on, and Grandpa banged around the kitchen for a while. Travis finished his math homework and worked on his word list. The TV went off.

"There's dinner on the stove," Grandpa yelled through the door. "I'm going to the meeting. I'll be home later."

Travis was on the couch when Grandpa came back.

"I called Chuck and it's a go," Grandpa said as he walked in the door. "I'll take you and your friend to the swamp Saturday. But just tell me this — are you going there to fool around? Because if you get her pregnant, I'll — "

"Grandpa! God! No."

Grandpa was as bad as Bradley. Worse.

"No sex, no drugs. Rock 'n' roll, that's fine."

"Forget the whole thing," said Travis. "It was a bad idea."

"I'll drop you for an hour or so and pick you up after."

Travis stared at the TV. Maybe it wasn't a bad idea. Even with Grandpa in the picture.

"What time you want to go?" asked Grandpa.

"I'll let you know. I gotta check with her."

"Her." Grandpa giggled. "You ever going to tell me the name of this her?"

"No."

Grandpa slapped his knee and lit up a cigarette.

Velveeta on TUESDAY

Since the madre didn't come to conferences, they gave me my mid-quarter grades today at school. It's the worst I've ever gotten. All Cs. I'd rather be almost anything than average. Calvin would give me sad eyes over this, and probably only let me watch black-and-white movies for a month.

I keep thinking about how Travis rescued Bradley from that punk Chilson and his buddies. I wish I could have seen it. I just love it that he protects Bradley. I liked that about him from the very first day.

I'd still love to see him beat the crap out of Jimmy. It can't ever happen because they'd have to be in the same place at the same time, and that would cause some freaky disruption to the space-time continuum of the universe. But it makes an amazing movie in my head. Best movie I've ever seen.

I've decided to quit the no-homework religion. It's no fun anyway since Travis converted. I took some books home and stopped by the library after school. Connie's teeth just about fell out of her head, she was so surprised.

Chapter Twenty-six

Travis found Velveeta in the lunchroom, eating a bowl of cereal.

"You get off at noon on Saturday, right?" he asked. "Are you busy after that?"

"Why, do you want to pull my wagon?"

"No, I want to take you someplace."

"Where?"

"It's a surprise. We'll be gone for like three hours. My grandpa's going to drive us. Do you want to?"

"That's a vague invitation." Velveeta got up and cleared her place. "Are you going to kidnap me and hold me for ransom?"

"No, but I have some words I need help with, and I thought we could do some of that."

"You're trying to help me by letting me help you. Don't think you're being tricky."

"I'm not being tricky. I just want to make sure you'll come." Travis followed Velveeta to her locker. "But you have to promise not to yell at me to try. If you do that, I'll leave."

"Let me get this right. You want me to go to some secret place with you, for some completely unexplained reason, and if I tell you to try, you'll walk away and leave me wherever we are."

"Right," said Travis as she closed her locker.

"That sounds like a perfect action-suspense setup. What time?"

"Anytime after one, because my grandpa works in the morning."

"One fifteen?"

"Okay, good. Wear warm clothes if it's cold, because we'll be outside."

"Is that a date?" Megan came up behind them as they entered the classroom. "Are Velveeta and Travis going on a date?"

"Pull your nose in, Megan," said Velveeta. "It's no date. It's a financial summit with our lawyers and accountants in Vegas. You can't come, so stop begging."

"Like I'd want to," said Megan.

"Yes, exactly like you'd want to."

Megan whispered to Cassidy on the other side of the classroom, and they both laughed.

"You're so mysterious," said Velveeta. "Okay, so probably not Vegas. But are we going to a secret hidden cave? *Indiana Jones*y?"

"No. Tell me where you live so we can pick you up."

"No. You can pick me up at the library."

Ms. Gordon closed the door, and Travis faced front, happy little birds fluttering around inside his chest. She said yes! This was going to be good.

"Okay, so you know Friday is the dance, right?" Bradley set his lunch down.

"Quit with the dance," said Travis.

"No, I know, I know. Not the dance. You're both invited to my house on Sunday for the anti-dance."

"Two invitations for Velveeta in one day," said Velveeta. "What's an anti-dance?"

"It's a party where nobody dances. I wanted it to be on Friday night, but my parents are busy. My dad said you can come Sunday afternoon for a while."

"Sunday afternoon — that's pretty anti-dance." Velveeta nodded. "Are your gamey pals coming?"

"No, they're going to the dance, so they can't anti-dance. It's just you and you and me. Travis, say yes and make her say yes."

"How am I supposed to do that?"

"Will there be food?" asked Velveeta.

"My mom said she'd make that spinach–pine nuts thing for a late lunch."

"Tempting. I'll think about it."

"Okay, this time that means yes, right? Oh, and Travis, she's going to make that cherry crisp thing that you liked last time you were over. Please? Say yes?"

"Don't beg, Bradley," said Velveeta. "Or we'll sic Chilson on you."

"I'm in," said Travis.

Bradley grinned so big, Travis thought the rubber bands on his braces might snap.

"I knew you would be. Come on, Velveeta, say yes."

"Okay, Bradley, yes. I will come to the anti-dance. If nothing else, just because you should be rewarded for thinking that party title up."

"Yay." Bradley gave a little hop in his seat and opened his lunch bag. "Two o'clock Sunday. My house."

When the bell rang, Travis walked with Velveeta to her locker.

"He's so Bradley-esque," she said. "You can't help liking that."

"He doesn't really care if we make fun of him, does he?" said Travis.

"No. I think he's adopted us, and the anti-dance is the official ceremony."

Velveeta on WEDNESDAY

When I got to the library today, Connie yanked me into the back room and held up a key. She said I needed a place to study and I could use the library when it's closed, but only under three conditions. Then she started jabbing the key in the air, a jab for each rule.

Jab number one: I can't tell anyone I have it, and if she ever hears about it from anyone else, she'll take it away from me. She said Pauline already knows, and Pauline's the only other one who has a key. So if anyone else ever knows, it's because I told them and key gone.

Jab number two: I have to lock the door when I'm in here. Always. If she ever comes and I'm here and the door isn't locked, key gone.

Jab number three: I can't ever bring anyone here with me. Because of course, that would also be breaking rule number one. Anyone here with me, key gone.

I told her it's not like I'm going to have crack parties in here. Maybe I'd just want Travis to come and study sometimes, and she said no, we can do that during open hours. No Travis, period, the end. Could I live with those rules, and did I want the key?

I asked her why she was so nice to me.

She said because Calvin was so nice to her.

I told her she is twisted.

And yes, I understood her rules, and yes, I want the key.

Chapter Twenty-seven

Travis turned the radio on and the volume up as he and Grandpa drove down the hill to pick up Velveeta.

"If you don't want me to say anything, just say so." Grandpa talked loud over the music.

"I'm saying so."

"Okay, I'll shut up."

Velveeta was waiting on the sidewalk in front of the library.

"There, pull over," said Travis.

"That's the girl? Velveeta is your her?"

Velveeta opened the truck door with a huge grin, and Grandpa turned the music down.

"Mr. Ed is not your grandpa. Tell me he's not. Mr. Ed, are you his grandpa?"

"Travis, you dog," said Grandpa. "Why didn't you tell me this was the girl you were talking about?"

Travis slid over so she could get in.

"Travis was talking about me?" Velveeta clicked the seat belt between her and Travis. "What did he say?"

"Not very much at all. Gotta drag words out of him with a backhoe and a crowbar."

"I know, right?" Velveeta laughed. "He only gives out ten a day. Fifteen on Fridays."

That was good for a big ol' hee-haw from Grandpa, but then he leaned over and turned the radio back up.

"Where are we going?" asked Velveeta.

Grandpa actually did not say anything. He stayed shut up.

"We're not talking now, are we?" Velveeta whispered in Travis's ear.

Travis shook his head, and Velveeta elbowed him in the side. They rode with nothing but music until Grandpa pulled over to the side of the road by the old place.

"You're dropping us in a ditch?" asked Velveeta.

"See you at three thirty, kids! Remember, Travis: only rock 'n' roll."

"What's that supposed to mean?" asked Velveeta as he drove off.

"Nothing. He's crazy. How do you know him, anyway?"

"I see him every Saturday at the bakery. He appreciates the Velveetic humor. Where are we going?"

"You'll see. Follow me."

The driveway was familiar but also completely different. A blue Prius instead of the truck. No Rosco row-wowing up to greet them. Travis kept his eyes turned away from the sunny spot on the gravel.

Just past the drive, trees closed in around them. Travis put his feet on his favorite dirt path, and the smells and sounds wrapped around him. Treetops murmured a soft and comforting conversation overhead. A red-winged blackbird tweedled the local gossip. Travis's skin stretched wide open, pulling it all in. He pointed at a pileated woodpecker that swept across the path in front of them. They both stopped and watched until it flew out of sight. The sun sprayed through the colors in the trees, and leaves drifted down in front of them.

"Oh, Travis," said Velveeta. "This is pretty."

"Remember you asked about a place? I'm taking you to it."

The path narrowed, and they couldn't walk side by side.

"So, you used to live by here?" Velveeta spoke softly behind him.

"Yup, in that house we just walked past. I came out here every day after school."

He turned at the fork, and the path widened as they

climbed the ridge near the swamp. The swamp water was as still and black as ever. Rusty pine needles layered the ground, along with shifting patterns of red and yellow leaves. Travis leaned against a birch trunk, and Velveeta sat next to him.

"Look at those yellow leaves on the water," she said. "They look like little boats. Why would you ever move away from here?"

"Kind of a long story."

"Oh. I know about those."

The sun shone on the stand of maples, firing up the opposite side of the swamp with red and orange like Velveeta's scarf that she didn't have anymore.

"So, will you tell me anything about anything?" asked Travis. "Like, what happened to your other scarves?"

"What's that noise?" asked Velveeta.

A high, throaty warble drifted across the treetops, growing louder.

"Sandhill cranes." Seven of them came into sight, big birds with necks stretched out straight and legs trailing behind. "Flying south."

The birds passed overhead in a V, hooting the whole way.

"Very *Jurassic Park*," said Velveeta as the sound faded. "I should have brought my lawyer friend. Maybe a T. rex would eat her."

"What lawyer friend?"

Silence settled around them, no sound but the breeze

rattling the leaves. Travis sat perfectly still like he used to do when waiting for a fox pup to stick its nose out of the den.

Velveeta lay back, looking up at the sky.

"This old guy Calvin lived next door to me," she said. "In a trailer. He was my best friend. I know that sounds like it might be skinky, but it's not. He gave me all those scarves. There were twenty-three of them. They used to be his wife's before she died. And then he went and died."

"When?"

"Forty-nine days ago."

Travis pulled Rosco's rabies tag out of his pocket. He rubbed it between his fingers.

"His daughter came back last week and kicked me out of the trailer and took the scarves. She's the lawyer I want to sic a dinosaur on."

"Why did she take them?"

"Because she is a manifestation of the forces of evil."

A woodpecker rattled, and Travis searched the treetops, trying to track the sound. It stopped, then started again, farther away.

"Can we get them back? I mean, maybe we could figure out a way."

"Nope," said Velveeta. "She lives in San Diego. The scarves are gone. Except this one because I was wearing it."

She stared up at the sky, rubbing the scarf between her fingers. Travis took the rabies tag off the key ring and handed it to her.

"Rabies vaccination?" She sat up to study it.

"I know it's not the same, but our dog, Rosco, died on August ninth. I mean, he's not a person or anything, but he was..."

What *was* Rosco? Mother father and a couple of brothers? Best friend? All that and more.

"August ninth this year? A Saturday?" Travis nodded. "That's exactly one week before Calvin died." She handed the tag back. "Calvin liked dogs. Maybe they're hanging out together."

"You think?"

A couple of birch leaves floated down into their own reflections in the black swamp water, more bright yellow boats in the harbor. Travis pulled *Haunt Fox* out of his backpack and opened to chapter two.

"See this?" He pointed at the line drawing of the hound. "That's what Rosco looked like."

"Oh..." Velveeta ran her fingertips across the picture.

"He had the softest ears ever. He was about the same color as your hair. Maybe a little more red."

Velveeta stroked the *Haunt Fox* dog's ears.

"Let's do some words," she said. "Or I'm going to get too sad."

"You sure? We don't have to do that."

"Yes, we do. Do you have a list?"

"I want to work on something else. Can you find the part where it talks about the puppy? It's in the second chapter."

Velveeta scanned through the pages.

"'He was a big, sad-eyed hound'?"

"Yeah, that. I want to learn all the words in that paragraph."

"It's a long paragraph. Look, it goes all the way to the next page."

Travis took the book from her and counted. Twenty-four circled words.

"Can you drill me through them all?"

He took out his notebook and pencil and handed them to her.

"You sure? You won't get mad?"

"As long as you don't tell me to just try."

Velveeta wrote down the words. She fed them to Travis, one at a time. Once they'd gone over the list a few times, he asked her to read the paragraph out loud.

He lay back on the ground as she turned the print on the page into a living dog, same as McQueen had done in his office. Travis had never known puppy-Rosco, and he never would. This was the next best thing.

When Velveeta finished the paragraph, he sat up. "Show me where it starts?" he said. "And read just that first sentence?"

She pointed at the words as she read. The string of print jumbled and shifted in front of him.

"Wait here," he said. "I'm going to go over there and try it by myself first."

"Is this the part where you run back to the truck and leave me alone in the woods?"

"No. I'm just going over there, by that tree. You can see me from here."

He sat with his back to her and looked at the words in the sentence one at a time, chewing through them slowly. He stuck with that first sentence, again and again, word by word.

"Travis," called Velveeta, "you okay over there?"

He nodded and drilled through the sentence again. Then he went back over and held the book up between them.

"Okay, you do it first. Just that sentence."

She read it. He followed with his eyes, imagining the yellow highlight from the Kurzweil moving across each word.

"Now you?"

Travis looked out at the swamp, taking in the hush of it, the breeze on his face, the crunchy smell and the soft carpet.

"See that stand of pines over there?" he said. "All the different greens? Just like your scarf."

"Here." Velveeta unwound the scarf. She put it around Travis's neck, and it settled soft and slidey on his skin. "It'll give you superpowers. Now read."

Travis gulped a big breath and plowed into the sentence. He kept tripping. He couldn't get through it.

"Wait, let's do the words again," said Velveeta.

They drilled words again, one at a time. Travis broke a sweat.

"Why do you want to do this?" he asked, taking a breather.

Velveeta lay back with her hands behind her head.

"Because it seems like I'm doing something real," she said. "That first time in the library, watching those words stick to your brain? That was so fun."

Travis lay next to her. The maple leaves blazed against the blue.

"Calvin would have liked you."

"Why?"

"He liked what I liked. We liked all the same movies. Anything he said was good, it was good. Even the black-and-white ones."

"What did he die of?"

"Heart attack. In his sleep. One day, boom, gone. No more Calvin."

Big puffer clouds moved slowly across the expanse of blue sky. The sun shone on Travis's face, warm but not hot.

"If it wasn't for him, I probably wouldn't know how to read, either. He always made me do my homework."

Travis felt like he could lie there all day listening to her talk, but Velveeta grabbed the shoulder of his shirt and pulled him up.

"Come on, try the sentence again."

"You said *try*," he said. "You're not supposed to say *try*."

"Sorry. I forgot. Don't try."

Travis sat up, took a breath, and shook himself loose.

Then he took the book from her and read the sentence all the way through. Not one stumble.

"Travis, that was so great!" yelled Velveeta. She held up her fist. "Pound it!"

Travis lifted his hand and tapped it gently against hers, and she caught his eyes and held them tight. Their knuckles stayed together, touching. The light hit her hair like it had that day by the garbage can, the deep brown-red of Rosco lying in the sun.

"What color do you call your eyes?" asked Velveeta. "Is that what they call hazel? Because they should have a whole different name for that color."

"I better check the time." Travis fumbled in his pocket for Grandpa's watch. "Uh-oh, we're late. Come on, we've got to run."

He shoved the book in his backpack and they took off. Travis couldn't have read another word, not after that. Velveeta's feet pounded behind his, along the dirt path and up the gravel drive to the road, where Grandpa was waiting in the truck.

Velveeta on a Sit-up SATURDAY

So I walked into the home trailer after the best day of my life so far and the madre did not even ask me where I'd been or did I have a good time. She told me Jimmy called and he's in Texas. Can this be true? I don't believe it. I think he's still in Russet and lying, but she had another drink.

I've been thinking about the whole sitter-upper thing that McQueen talked about from *The Book Thief.* The madre is not a sitter-upper. She's a lier-downer. But Travis is a sitter-upper.

If it wasn't for him, I would have turned into a lier-downer after Calvin died. Or for sure after Sylvia took my scarves. I don't want to be a lier-downer. Even if I never get out of Russet for my whole life. I'll be a sitter-upper waitress if I have to.

Chapter Twenty-eight

Travis met Velveeta at the corner of Water Street.

"Travelli," she said. "We are going to a party at Bradley Whistler's, right? Pinch me and tell me I'm not in some wacky nightmare."

"You're not. See? That's his house at the end of the block. That brick one with the white trim."

"Oh, and there's Bradley, just coming out to look for us. Look at him — he's so excited."

Bradley herded them in the front door and introduced Velveeta to his folks. Everyone said good to meet you, and they sat down to the spinach–pine nuts stuff for lunch. Travis picked around the green and orange and ate the pasta. There was plenty of fresh bakery bread and homemade applesauce, and cherry crisp for dessert. Much better than bakery day-olds.

Velveeta started off quiet, but by the time they got to dessert, she loosened up.

"Okay, wait, watch this," she said. "Watch me — I'm Bradley." She knocked on the table. "Hey, open up. What's the password? What's the password, roger roger? I'm the Master Chief — give me the password. That's the password. What's the password? The password is the password."

"No, no," yelled Bradley, laughing. "It's 'Oh, man, I forgot.' Then it goes — "

She knocked on the table again. "I'm Bradley of the supersonic brain. Open the door. I don't need no frickin' password. Just hook my games back up right now. Come on, hand them over or I'll neutralize your whole squad."

Bradley's parents totally cracked up. They laughed way harder than Travis could see what was funny, and Bradley's mom actually snorted water out her nose.

"Velveeta, you're good," said Bradley's dad, still trying to get his breath. "You kids go on and do your anti-dance thing. We can't take any more."

Travis and Velveeta followed Bradley upstairs. His room was big enough to put three or four of Travis's bedroom in it.

"Why do you have two computers, Bradley?" asked Velveeta. "Do you type on a different one with each hand?"

"No, that's one of my mom's old ones. She lets me take it apart and mess with it. I'm the family IT department."

"No TV in your room? Of course, with a big flat-screen like that one downstairs, who needs it?"

"I used to have one in here, but my dad took it on his anti-electronics binge. I'm lucky he let me keep the computers and my phone. I told him it'd be good if we could play when you guys came over, but he said I can't contaminate you in this house."

"Bradley Whistler contaminating me," said Velveeta. "That's a walk into backward land. Look at all these books. Have you read them all?"

She walked along the full-wall bookshelf, trailing her fingers across the spines.

"Mostly." Bradley sat on the floor.

"You could open your own library," said Velveeta.

Travis sat near Bradley and leaned against the dresser.

"So, Travis," said Velveeta, "why does Cormick call you Moolio, anyway?"

"He says Travis is one coolio moolio," said Bradley. "That's way better than Chocolate Chip."

"Chocolate Chip was not Chad's best effort. Velveeta, on the other hand, was a stroke of genius."

"Chad named you that?" asked Travis.

"Back in second grade. Chad can't call anyone by just their name. It's a speech impediment. Do you like Moolio?"

"Beats Bluefish."

"Bluefish? What's that?" asked Bradley.

"They called me that at my old school. Because of the reading group I was in, back in third grade."

Bradley bounced up and pulled a book off the shelf. He pointed at the cover.

"This, right? Your groups were One Fish, Two Fish, Red Fish, Blue Fish?"

The dumb bluefish stared at Travis with that stupid blank idiot smile.

"But look!" said Velveeta. "That bluefish is the moolio fish. He's all cazh, kicking back on a wave while One and Two and Red are swimming around like a herd of water sheep."

"I want to be a bluefish," said Bradley.

"You can't," said Travis. "You're too smart."

"No, no." Velveeta took the book from Bradley and pointed at the picture. "Look at how the bluefish will not swim when the others swim. The bluefish is at the anti-dance."

She leaned against the shelf in the same pose as the bluefish leaning on the wave, hand on hip, smiling the big close-lipped smile. Only it didn't look stupid on her — it looked like she was up to something.

"See? I'm a bluefish."

"Wait, me too!" Bradley leaned on his desk and popped his eyes wide open and smiled like a maniac. "Am I doing it right?"

"You don't want to." Travis shook his head, laughing.

"Yes, we do," said Velveeta. "We're here, we're anti-dancing, we're bluefish. I think we should have tattoos. Bradley, do you have a blue pen?"

Bradley tossed her a blue marker from his desk. She drew the fish picture on the back of her hand.

"That looks more like a fat worm than a fish," said Bradley.

"Okay, you're so good, let's see you draw one. Put it on Travis's hand there."

Travis held out his fist, and Bradley drew the fish. It was much better than Velveeta's.

"Look at the long eyelashes on that thing!" said Velveeta. "Bradley, I had no idea you were all artistic. Put one on your own hand."

Bradley took a long time to draw his own. Finally, he held his hand up.

"Look, it hardly shows on me," he said.

"That's because you're a stealth bluefish," said Velveeta. "Cleverly disguised as a onefish. Look, we can even have a secret bluefish wave."

She rippled her hand through the air, dipping it up and down like it was riding ocean waves.

"Everyone wants to be a bluefish, but we're a very select group. We need a password and a secret handshake. We should make up a bluefish code. Everyone will want to be us."

"Hey, kids." Bradley's dad knocked. "It's going on

four. Travis, Velveeta, get your shoes on. I'm taking you home."

"You don't need to drive us home. We can walk," said Velveeta as Bradley's dad opened the door.

"You sure?" he asked. "It's no trouble."

"We'd rather walk, right, Travis?" said Velveeta. Travis nodded. "It's not raining or anything."

They followed Bradley's dad downstairs. Travis and Velveeta thanked Bradley's parents, and everyone said how much fun it was.

"That actually was fun," said Velveeta once they got up the street a ways.

"Yeah, it was. How come you never let anybody drive you home? You even made us drop you off at the library yesterday."

Layers of clouds blanketed the sky, and a chilly wind blew them along. Velveeta wrapped the ends of her scarf around her neck and tucked them inside her hoodie.

"Mr. Noticer Boy, are you sure you're not an undercover cop?"

"Even if Mr. Whistler drove us, you'd make him drop you at the library, right?"

"Right. So listen, I've been thinking about Rosco's rabies tag. Does carrying it with you make you feel like Rosco is less dead?"

"Not really." Travis found the tag in his pocket. "I mean, if anything, it makes him feel more dead because if he were alive, then he'd be wearing it, not me."

"Right." She unwound her scarf a couple of turns and wrapped one end around her palm. "This is different. I'd be wearing it even if Calvin were still alive."

"But carrying it with me . . ." Travis pressed the tag, flat and warm, into the center of his palm. "It doesn't make him not dead, but it makes him not as much gone, you know? Like sometimes when I rub it, I can sort of smell him."

Velveeta rubbed the scarf across her cheek. They came to Main Street, but instead of turning toward town, Velveeta stepped onto the bridge and leaned over the railing. The water looked cold and choppy in the wind, and leaves swirled down and hit the surface.

"So it's not like you're someone who never had a Rosco, right? So even though Calvin's dead, it's not like I'm someone who never had a Calvin. Because if there'd been no Calvin, there'd be no scarf."

"Yeah," said Travis. "Not that scarf, anyway. I mean, you could go buy some other scarf, like I could go get another rabies tag. But you couldn't get that one."

"Even with all the scarves gone but this one, I can't turn into a no-Calvin Velveeta. Like you can never be a no-Rosco Travis, right?"

"Right."

The water rushed beneath them. Travis picked up a stick and threw it in. It drifted toward the bridge, picking up speed as it got close to the dam. When it went under, they ran across and watched it come out the other side.

The stick hurtled over and crashed into the white water at the bottom.

"So I was wondering," said Velveeta. "Is there a Mrs. Ed?"

"Nope. She died before I was born."

"What about Ed Junior? Or Edwina?"

"My dad died when I was three. So did my mom." Velveeta opened her mouth, but Travis stopped her. "It's okay. I hardly remember them."

He picked up another stick, crossed the road, and threw it as far as he could. The wind and the current pushed it swiftly toward the dam. He crossed back over and leaned next to Velveeta.

"So you don't miss them?" she asked.

"No. Not like Rosco."

The stick shot over the falls and disappeared into the foam and rocks at the bottom. Travis leaned farther over the railing, looking for it to pop up again. Velveeta pointed at the bluefish Bradley had drawn on his hand.

"Did you mind?" she asked. "Us getting all bluefishy with it?"

"No, it's fine," said Travis. "It's different here."

"That's because you've got me and Bradley in your school. Ha. Get it, your school?"

"Ha," said Travis.

The stick finally resurfaced near the steep bank, floated downstream on smooth, fast-running water, and disappeared around the curve.

"Hey, speaking of school, have you been practicing that sentence so you can wow McQueen tomorrow?"

"I've got the first two down now."

"Can I come and watch you wow him?"

"No."

"Please?"

"No."

"Fine, cut me out of the good part. That's just like you." She pushed away from the railing. "I'd better get going. See you tomorrow, Travarelli."

About a block away, she turned around and walked backward. She rolled her left hand up and down in the bluefish wave. Travis bluefish-waved back. She flipped the end of her scarf at him, turned around, and walked on.

Travis leaned over the railing and held his fist out over the rolling water. The smile wasn't all that stupid. It was kind of quiet and happy. And the way the fish leaned on the wave was, maybe, a little bit moolio.

Travis opened his fist, and dipped his hand up and down in the bluefish wave, skimming and diving over the surface of the water.

"Fsssssshhh."

ACKNOWLEDGMENTS

Many thanks to those who have helped bring *Bluefish* into the world by sharing their experience, reading drafts, offering ideas, and generally supporting me and the book in a variety of creative ways: Alice Deighan, Andrew Karre, Annetta Wright, Catherine Friend, Deb Gordon, Dwyer Deighan, e.E. Charlton-Trujillo, Jane St. Anthony, Jane Resh Thomas, Jeremy Schmatz, Kim Swineheart, Laura Greene, Lisa Cohen, Ned Cohen, Nora Frala, Rachel Gordon, Ruth Gordon, Robin Stevenson, Ruth Schmatz, and Taylor Gordon.

I'm very grateful for the generosity of Phyllis Reynolds Naylor and the PEN American Center.

Thank you to Joan Powers, my editor at Candlewick, for her insight, guidance, and direction.

And finally, thanks to my agent, Andrea Cascardi, who has supported *Bluefish* over many years and multiple forms. I deeply appreciate her patience and keen editorial eye.

NORTH HIGH SCHOOL LIBRARY
Sheboygan, WI 53083